MW01226980

GREEN LEAVES GIFTED

TOGHRA GHAEMMAGHAMI

 FriesenPress

Victoria, BC, V8V 3K2
Canada
www.friesenpress.com

ISBN

978-1-03-910424-2 (Hardcover)
978-1-03-910423-5 (Paperback)
978-1-03-910425-9 (eBook)

1. Fiction, Short Stories (Single Author)

Distributed to the trade by The Ingram Book Company

TABLE OF CONTENTS

Relying on the Kindness of Strangers: Kindness in the Balkans

Of all the good plays by the tormented playwright Tennessee Williams, I have only grabbed one phrase. It's from *A Streetcar Named Desire*, and is pronounced by the lips of a madwoman: "Whoever you are, I have always depended on the kindness of strangers."

Tennessee Williams did not enjoy any form of intimacy but his observation of the negative aspects of human life was razor sharp. In the play, Blanche Dubois, overcome by her own fragility and the brutality of those around her, has retreated into a state of fantasy and madness. This phrase depicts the height of mistrust and alienation.

In my experience, however, the phrase also underlines the immense potential for goodwill in humans. I have been the unwitting recipient of goodness from total strangers on numerous occasions.

One of my destinations in the Balkans was Dracula Castle. Years ago, I had heard from a young lady from Transylvania that it's really eerie and that, as soon as you get close to it, you feel spirits moving around you. Up to that moment, Dracula for me was just a fictional character in a book turned to a movie, which scared me to death when I was a child.

Now in the Balkans and so close to it, I did what I always do: enjoy the visual experience, engage in an emotional handshake with the locals, and walk on the earth. No need to study history or geography.

After a bus ride or two and a train ride, I found myself in a small, quaint medieval town called Brasov, in the centre of Transylvania, in the northern part of Romania, where a tourist map said Dracula Castle was in the vicinity. To my mind, that meant next to the train station. Although I had started early in the morning, it was already around 5 p.m., and I would be leaving at 6 a.m. the next morning from the same station, destined for Piran. I had planned to get a hotel near the castle, leave my carry-on there, and visit the castle. But there was no castle in my sight. So, I started to use human Google. Nobody had heard of Dracula Castle. Kind strangers who could barely understand or speak English were finally able to decode what I was looking for. I soon learned it was known to locals as Bran Castle. And it was located in a little village two hours away, which would require two bus transfers. I went toward the bus stop and kept saying the word Bran to people, make it sure I was in the right place. A kind lady waved her hands, inviting me to stay beside her. The bus arrived and she pointed her ticket to me. I showed her my money for a bus ticket. Her panicky face alerted me that, as is the case in most European cities, the ticket should have been bought from the train station. The lady however gestured me to go in. She pushed me away from the driver and sat me on a vacant chair before sitting herself next to me. I noticed during the almost one-hour drive and the many stops on rural roads that she was making the repeated sign of the cross, and from the corner of her eyes, throwing reassuring glances at me. Each time I got up to go to the driver to offer the money she would push me back into my seat. I did not know what was happening. I knew there was a penalty for dodging the fare. If I were asked to leave the bus, I would be left in the middle of nowhere. The lady wrote something on her ticket. And then bus stopped and she almost ran out, pushing her ticket into my palm, and pointing forward, indicating I should get out at the next station and board another bus.

I stepped down in an out-of-town crossroad. Just dirt roads. A bus was standing at a corner. I looked at the ticket and her written number was the same as the bus. I entered and gave my ticket to the bus driver and he let me sit. The bus was almost full and it departed after less than two minutes. I had gotten on it by the skin of my teeth through the kindness of the local lady. Had she given me her transfer? Did she get out to buy herself a new ticket as she knew it would be difficult for me and that I may lose my ride? I'll never know. But I realized that being a pious Christian, she had done a bad thing by helping me to cheat and was praying for forgiveness.

The rural road slowed the drive through pristine green fields and as we were approaching Bran, the August sun was setting in a hurry. When we arrived, it was 9 p.m. From the window I saw the formidable castle standing on a huge rock on a hill across the street for a few seconds before dark replaced dusk. On the rock a large face of a wolf with an open mouth was carved. The driver said something and then looked at me and said, "Nine morning!" No way! My train will be leaving at 6 a.m.

But I said to myself: Well, that's Dracula Castle, so leave now. I said to the bus driver that I would go back to Brasov. He waved and said, "No!" He was going home, not to Brasov.

I stepped out in a panic and the bus left.

It was a darkened village with a variety store close to me and, across the street, a bar and a guesthouse with colourful lights.

I noticed a man and his little boy standing near the variety store talking on the phone. I approached him and, with mime, gestures, and words, said I wanted to go back to Brasov. He immediately gave me a reassuring wave and called on his phone. I thanked him.

In a short time, a taxi in poor shape with a passenger in the front appeared. The kind man went to the driver and talked to him, then opened the cab door for me. I thanked him pitifully.

The passenger was the driver's wife, and both were in their early twenties. She could speak English as she had worked as a housekeeper and nanny for an English family in Italy. Her husband worked in a factory during the day and drove at night. The drive to Brasov was almost two hours, all in blackness save the elegant moonshine and plenty of stars. She accompanied him to be together. They were both working hard to save money for her dental work. After that, they will have children. She said malnutrition in childhood caused tooth decay. Some of her front teeth were missing. During the ride she reserved a room for me in a tiny motel that was a five minutes' walk to the train station so I'd be OK for the 6 a.m. departure. The jet-black road was a world away from our tender conversation.

They carried my carry-on to the tiny motel. I took a photo of them and we embraced and parted.

Bram Stoker had not seen Bran Castle—only its drawings. I imagined the blood-sucking Dracula from real Vlad as a bloodthirsty Impaler, a powerful political force of the fifteenth century in Bran. Vlad's castle, now ruined, was in another province. The wolf carved on the rock was an optical illusion! It was just solid boulders. People in Bran actually believe in the "undead" and moving spirits.

In a short time, I was going to Split, a medieval port city in Croatia on an uneven land. A medieval castle, a busy tourist attraction was put on sale. Split had many attractive islands, Dalmatian. I wanted to go to the nearest one, and left my B&B place early in the morning to walk toward the harbour and ferry port just across the road. The square was clear, only a VW passed me. I was walking fast and heard somebody calling. I kept my pace and the voice was getting closer and louder. I looked back and saw a young woman running and waving toward me, yelling, "Madame! Madame!" I stopped and when she reached me, she handed over a fist-sized transparent pouch filled with folded Croatian money. She was the driver of the VW and had noticed that I dropped something in my hurried state. She had parked the car in the middle of the street, picked up the pouch, and run after me.

I got a ferry to Supetar and had a delicious lunch facing the beautiful blue Adriatic Sea. And all thanks to the kindness of a stranger. Blanche Dubois knew what she was talking about.

Thirty Birds . . . Simurgh

When I arrived in Canada in 1969, in one sense it was like visiting a neighbour's house.

I was just absorbed by all that was unfamiliar. The absorption by the unfamiliar was buffered by all the utterly familiar. My field of study gave me the good luck of feeling at home with friends and colleagues. It was like being cuddled by loving members of my family.

Yet the unfamiliarity was so exciting that it seemed that I'd ditched my past somewhere outside of my awareness and gobbled up the newness.

Canada's youth and its short history involving the forceful segregation of First Nations, and the shameful treatment of their children, was nothing compared with thousands of years of documented history of the blood- and pride-soaked Persian Empire. Ontario's flat earth was far from the mountainous land I had roamed. Its sky with few stars was in stark contrast to the star-studded cerulean sky of Iran. And its literature and poetry were in abject poverty compared to the literary medium in which I had bathed. Yet I put away the past, and grabbed the roots of this new home. My next-door neighbour. Latin, Greek, Russian, German, French, and English were in the DNA of my education, but now they were like story-time tales.

It took me a few decades to swim back to my roots and let myself be embraced by what had made my earlier molecules.

Poetry, the immortal part of literature, is indeed the oxygen breathed in from the time Persian ears can hear. At the risk of being identified as an arrogant person, I declare Farsi to be one of the best mediums for poetry. Like the best marble for sculpting.

The same way skies, nowadays only in villages, were studded by millions of stars, poets are a major product of the Iranian literary machine. It's in the blood. No air pollution can tarnish it, and it fades away, the way it happens to the stars. Just momentarily.

Every single poet gives a unique rendition of life and its vicissitudes. The immensity is awesome. I would never compare one with another. I'm just lucky to have heard a few lines from each poem, to have sampled the ultra-delicious, highly nutritious supplement.

Revisiting the past, I came upon Attar, a humble poet working as an assistant in his father's apothecary shop in northeast Iran in the thirteenth century. His pursuit of spirituality devoid of religiosity brought him the label of sophist. Sophist in Farsi has Greek roots. It is a seeker of wisdom and truth. But, somehow, a lack of religious pretension allows for a negative slant, when religion is functioning as a political force.

But poets roll on the pages of time unscathed. And become immortal. Attar had the gift. Without looking for the laurel crown, the way Dante laboured.

In his rich endowment to humanity, his "Four Liners" and "the Conference of Birds" shine with blinding intensity.

Long before Attar, Persian mythology introduced a powerful bird called Thirty Birds, who acted like an advisor and saviour at once and as a personal helicopter for the national hero Rostam. Rostam is not just physically powerful like Hercules. He is a nationalist. And Simurgh, Thirty Birds, is always at his service in the most difficult times. When Simurgh notices that Rostam may go blind, he offers Rostam a long ride to get the medicine from a faraway land, across the China sea. According to our nannies' stories, Rostam got far more rides than that. But I have to respect the immortal work of Ferdowsi, "Shahnameh" in which Rostam gets only one ride.

The central theme in Conference of Birds is a search for Simurgh, as a way of searching for spirituality.

The story starts with birds of all feathers gathering in the forest and lamenting the lack of a cohesive personal identity and social network. They feel deprived compared with other creatures in the wild.

Hoopoe (HodHod in Farsi) arrives with good news.

The beautiful, colourful bird not bigger than a blue jay is native to Africa and most of Asia. Actually, its song sounds like "Hoopoe."

Why has HodHod been endowed with wisdom and the ability for guidance from time immemorial? From the Old Testament to Quranic verses, HodHod is the messenger to prophet Solomon.

In Conference of Birds, he does his ultimate guidance.

He has the answer to the ailments of birds. He knows a leader in a faraway mountain who can heal the spiritual woes of rudderless birds.

Learning of the hard journey and far distance from their tour guide makes birds bow out from their ambitious undertakings, one by one, with different excuses.

HodHod, however, with an impeccable logic and the keenness of a skilled tour operator, breaks their resistance and they embark. Here, Attar displays his deep knowledge of the bird kingdom.

The journey is too hard and the birds keep wanting to give up, but HodHod nudges them forward.

At the height of their confusion and not knowing which direction is the right one, HodHod informs and enlightens them that there are as many ways as birds to reach their destination. Each has to trust their own path, one that is compatible with their limitations and strength. They forge on. That is, those who survive forge on. Many perish.

At last, the surviving birds arrive at the impossible summit and enter the space to meet Thirty Birds, Simurgh.

There, they see their own reflection. There are exactly thirty birds. They cry in protest to HodHod, "Where is Simurgh, our leader? We only see ourselves."

HodHod informs them that, all along, the leader was in themselves, but they could not have trusted the inner strength without having actually assuaged it and put it to the test.

Attar could have been executed for turning people away from their imagined god somewhere out there. Even though he said it through the medium of birds, his intention to activate spirituality was only too clear. Attar was murdered by accident.

I am still searching for my inner Simurgh.

THE BLOOD-SOAKED NUTMEG TRADE AND OUR PURSUIT OF MAGIC

I like riches, wealth, and the courage to get it. Yes, Bill Gates! Great wealth seems to always arrive through some sort of business. Never through a profession.

There is a lot of risk-taking in business. Not like my neck of the woods, where every step involves a serious deliberation. Looking back, though, taking risks was in my territory, too, without admitting to it. And deliberation is also part of business, such as creating false scarcity, its bread and butter through human history. The fascinating accounts of trade at times where no easy navigation was possible by land or sea (and air only in imagination through magic carpets in stories), tell us how human ingenuity is at work at all times. The Chinese Road, Silk Road, and Royal Road are ancient paths that traders etched to take their merchandise as far as their mobility system allowed.

The earlier Spice Road goes back 3,000 years, to a time when Arabs were the main traders. (Arabs are not only smart with oil and taking huge space in medical schools in Canada.) By the time of the rise of Islam, Turks got the monopoly.

The spices sought through trade were branded mostly by their medicinal properties. Traders had kept the location of the source of the spices a secret. By the sixteenth century, Europe had become enriched by imported spices and Venice had a monopoly on their distribution. By land and by sea, the competition for this trade had become fierce.

By the seventeenth century, nutmeg had become the new icon, a new conduit to wealth-building that could cure even the plague. It was so expensive that all rich folks had to display it on their table. Pepper and salt have had their own days of ruling. The glorious underground salt mine in Krakow, Poland, is a testimony to the empire of salt, which lasted from the thirteenth to the twentieth century.

Nutmeg's glory lasted a few hundred years, too.

Everybody knew about the abundance of spice in India, but the whereabouts of the best nutmeg had remained a secret. Portuguese navigators were the first to find out about some small islands in Indonesia that were producing the best nutmeg. Indeed, they made a deal with locals and started exporting nutmeg. But soon Dutch traders and their sophisticated navy arrived and ousted the Portuguese. This was in the early seventeenth century. The Dutch do everything perfectly. It's in their genes. They took the distribution power from Venice. They colonized the Banda Islands, and made the rule that the slightest indiscretion, including selling nutmeg by local workers, would be penalized by execution.

Within a few years, by 1621, the Dutch had massacred the populations of Ai and Run islands, the main plantation site for the evergreen trees that produce nutmeg. Of 15,000 people, only 600 were kept alive to continue farming with the help of imported slaves. Commander Jan Coen still has his celebrated statue in Holland. His political savvy released Dutch colonists from relentless attacks by the British navy hoping to win nutmeg war. Coen muted the British by giving them the newly colonized almost uninhabitable Island in the New World called New Amsterdam—the present-day Manhattan.

He made Holland ultra-rich by selling overpriced nutmeg.

The Dutch monopoly of the nutmeg trade lasted almost 150 years—long enough to produce blue-blooded aristocrats far from the blood-soaked origins of the nutmeg trading business. It ended in 1769 when a French missionary, Pierre Poivre, outsmarted the Dutch traders and stole some nutmeg seeds and trees and planted them on Mauritius Island. Nutmeg was scarce no longer.

Take a bit and it is good, but take a lot and you can die. Even I, with my tendency to overuse everything, use nutmeg only in small quantities. Indeed, I happily substitute it with humble, not-too-well-known allspice, which is shaped like a large peppercorn and has a multilayered fragrance.

My fondness for business has never dimmed, despite negative goings-on. One of the recent deliberations to enhance business was accomplished through Loblaws apparently fixing the price of bread, the staple of many Canadian families.

When it comes to luxury items and, apparently, scarce commodities, my tolerance for price fixing is high.

Talking about scarcity, it could be true or false. For false scarcity, my blood comes to a boil fast. Like having to pay exorbitant prices for worthless medications that fuel hope in people's hearts that, somehow, their compromised health will be restored. The magic of nutmeg comes in many forms.

The Dutch reluctantly apologized in 2012 for their genocide of the Javanese in 1947. They haven't apologized for the Banda Islands, however. Not that Canada has been better. It took Canada a painfully long time to admit to its attempts to culturally annihilate natives.

A new push for reconciliation can be seen in the removal of the statue of the first Canadian prime minister, a perpetrator of dark deeds to First Nations people, from the city hall in Victoria, British Columbia.

And the pope, the CEO of one of the most successful trades, selling magic, has not yet admitted to the crimes its glamorous courtiers committed.

In the centre of the city state of Singapore, there is a new sculpture of nutmeg the size of a small room on a bygone nutmeg plantation.

I prefer this form of acknowledgement to destroying the efforts of a sculptor because the subject of his arduous artwork was retrospectively demonized. The latter smacks of another form of black magic.

MACHU PICCHU, GOD'S HOLIDAY DESTINATION

The first time I heard "Machu Picchu," I thought, people who are so passionately talking about it have made a funny word. But the joy in their faces was far away from talking about something funny.

I was on a Galapagos Island tour and, as usual, was disappointed to be in a cruise. Too much food. My tour mates, however, were people who had a vast history of travelling the world. And it was very interesting to listen to their experiences.

My attention was frozen on the word Machu Picchu without knowing its spelling or the accompanied joy. It became an instant destination for me, without learning a word about it.

I was more than happy to find a hiking tour straight from Toronto, run by a seventy-year-old German-born experienced hiker. I registered for a two-week hike immediately. And shortly before the trip I started to study the mailed brochures and tour itinerary. In every email, the tour operator indicated that we wouldn't need hiking boots—just normal walking shoes. We were advised to just make sure we had protection against very high elevation when we landed in Lima, and a bit more in Cusco. And of course, to watch for local dysentery. He also repeatedly pleaded to bring an old suitcase filled with unwanted new men clothing for the Peruvian workers.

For some reason, I had decided to take my hiking boots. I had been among life-long hikers and knew I was a total novice.

In the airport gathering prior to departure the tour leader, dressed in a light beige Tilley, was a tall, well-built man with a greying blonde crew cut that was very neat looking, true to his German origin. He was polite but basically very aloof and of few words. He said it was his twenty-fourth time going to Machu Picchu, and that he'd hiked many other parts of the world. But no mountain is as beautiful as the Andes in that area.

The group of fifteen were all seasoned hikers, but it was everybody's first time. They were all very personable types.

In Lima, our group was reduced to twelve. Three were throwing up so badly that they'd decided to return to Toronto. The next day we were reduced to ten after a white water rafting tragedy took one traveller's life and sent another to hospital, before we started seven nights and eight days on a camping/hiking expedition. The populated clean mountainous terrain with seamless green was one of the most treacherous paths I had ever been on. Incan paths were almost vertical to deter invaders. The industrious culture, savvy in producing food had had to protect itself from less fortunate neighbours in centuries past.

Whether it was caused by Montezuma's revenge, elevation sickness or the tragedy, I was sick as a dog the entire time. Yet I continued hiking thanks to my hiking boots, all the time seeing the German with his walking shoes and light beige Tilley outfit and hat soldiering ahead of all and arriving at least half an hour earlier that the rest. Our group was entirely managed by a hired tour guide and his men. Except at dinner time when the German would socialize with us, he was on his own with no sense of responsibility. Only a few times he talked about the tragedy, feeling sorry. Never regretful.

As for me, severe dehydration and an electrolyte imbalance caused such weakness that, on one occasion, I had to be carried on a horse, with no harness, while a helper walked the horse. Left to myself I would have been five hours behind, deep in the darkness and magical starry sky. On the horse I saw my death helplessly all the while.

By the third day of hiking, we were reduced to five. The other five had decided to make a shortcut and take the train to Cusco and wait for us.

Every day we started to climb around 6:30 a.m., after breakfast, and before dark, we arrived at a designated campground where our individual tents were set up, with a bowl of hot water to wash up before dinner. Lunch was served somewhere at midday. The path was peopled by numerous tours and independent tourists. A few times a person on a stretcher looking totally exhausted was carried down to the nearest village.

Night was the most difficult time. After all day perspiring under beautiful, caressing sun rays and a flawless blue sky, at night we had to sleep in sub-zero temperatures with the help of hot water bottles and wearing several layers of winter clothing. The hygienic aspect of our journey due to makeshift outhouses (which had to be dug for the night and filled the next morning after our departure, due to strict Peruvian government law), lack of proper bathing, lack of running water, grew increasingly worse.

The beautiful landscape, joyful climb and hike, myriad winking, brilliant stars in the night sky, were all lost on me due to my sickness and broken spirit. There was also increasing tension among the group, although we stayed civilized.

And then there were cheers when we arrived at a place God would choose for a holiday. It was just an impression in my mind.

It was an unmatched green sculpted in the form of a dense, forested mountain with a few shorter peaks, surrounding the remains of an ancient civilization hugged by blue heaven.

A short walk downhill, not vertical, and we were at Cusco, meeting the five who had left and the one who had been discharged from hospital.

I met a number of hikers from different tours, and independent tourists who had climbed the same path but in a much better way: with well-built, heated cabins with showers, toilets, and running water facilities in their campgrounds. And at a lower price. I felt bilked.

I was wondering if our suitcases with unwanted new men clothing were part of his payment to hired locals. I still question how our tour operator kept his light beige outfit so clean, without even a smudge? While the rest of us looked totally disheveled. How did he walk so fast with his walking shoes on those vertical paths? At seventy. Not bad, eh?

My sickness stayed until I arrived in Toronto. But the beauty of Machu Picchu is tattooed in my memory.

THE COWARD DIES
A THOUSAND TIMES
BEFORE HIS DEATH, BUT
THE VALIANT TASTES
OF DEATH BUT ONCE

River rules.

In the evening of our arrival in Lima, there was a meeting about the next morning's plan. After giving a free pisco sour to each of us, the local tour leader introduced himself and two young brothers with years of experience as surfing and rafting instructors in California. They had come back to Peru recently and we were very lucky to have them as leaders for our white water rafting. They would teach us how to use oars to stay synchronized!!!

I was nearly shocked, but although his English was flawless, I preferred to think he was making a linguistic mistake. It was river rafting, right? I corrected. He said firmly, confirmed by our German tour operator, "It's white water rafting—of course it's in a river. Very exciting."

Even pisco sour could not have numbed my brain enough to stop me from protesting—me, who had never mastered taking an oar in her hand, never mind rowing with it; me, who had seen white water rafting only in movies and heard of its life-threatening dangers first-hand from people who loved to flirt with death. For me, no persuasion would work. My campaign to get excused started. I declared loud and clear that, although I was a good swimmer even in oceans, my incapability borders on disability to negotiate an oar in calm Lake Muskoka or Rice Lake, or Bear Lake, or whatever tame water. And also, there was no mention of white water rafting in our itinerary, just river rafting.

Some of the hikers nodded. One was a pleasant, fit, small-built lady, Ann, who, sitting beside me, repeated my concern but much less dramatically. We had a few minutes to chat. She told me she was from England, sixty, and childless, and just the year before had retired with her corporate husband in Collingwood after years of travelling in North America. She was a good swimmer but her experience in boating was limited to going for a ride on their yacht in Lake Simcoe.

More than the Peruvian guide, it was Ann's friend who tried hard to dissolve our fears. She was practically born into violent Pacific water, being from Australia, and an avid surfer and rafter all her life. She and her husband also had retired to Collingwood and happened to be a neighbour of Ann's. She was sitting at the other side of Ann trying to nudge her away from my negative persistence. The Guides collectively laughed heartily about our unnecessary concern and kept reassuring us that we would see how easy and fun it would be. The German was unfazed. All looked convinced but me. I was not going.

In Thailand we had river rafting, too. It was child's play on a wide, shallow, tame stream hugged by greenery and bamboo branches. The raft was made from sturdy bamboo branches, roped together into a large, flat, five-metre-by-two-metre rectangular surface with an expert Thai rafter standing in front leading it with a long bamboo stick, while each containing six hikers sitting relaxed at the middle. The guides had to create speed for the raft to move on. They made it exciting by simulating bumps through their skilled method making the raft momentarily tilted. And we would playfully scream. One hour of it.

The Peruvian guide came to me and reassured me that I will not be doing any rowing just sit there and enjoy it as two experts are leading the rafts. Looking back, now I think that our German tour guide was going to pay him by the number of people he could take, and he did not want to shortchange himself.

That night I was awoken by commotion and noise. My roommate was violently sick. I gave her Diamox but it did not help. In the morning two more people had altitude sickness. The three of them decided to go back to Toronto. Had they seen their death by prospect of rafting in River Rímac, "the speaking river"?

The next morning after arriving at the mooring, which looked shallow and motionless, we were given wetsuits and caps and shoes. I'll never forget how proud Ann looked in her perfect fit, and the brave face she presented to me to relieve my fears. I barely fit into my wetsuit.

Two young men took the helm of one plastic raft and the six like me who had declared lack of experience were given to the more skilled rafter. Ann went with her expert friend. Our leader told us how to hold the oar and follow his instructions for forward and backward strokes. As soon as we left the mooring, the Pacific-like currents took over. It was exactly like what had frightened me in the movies. They were too rapid and powerful and they seemed running over either blackholes or enormous rocks on the riverbed, which sucked them in or launched them forward, making our raft nearly capsize every few seconds, each time, our leader making a loud, triumphant sound. The more experienced rafters in front screamed collectively with a ring of excitement each time their raft regained balance. I was no longer holding the raft or oar firmly, as if I was feeling safer swimming than thrashing about in a capsized raft. Or I had given up any hope to survive. Like the coward in *Julius Caesar*, I was dying a thousand times before my death. And valiant Ann tasted death but once. Within half an hour or much less, though it felt like an eternity, right before my eyes, the raft ahead of us capsized. I saw the heads of people floating and disappearing, and heard the occasional scream. Our leader immediately moored the raft and instructed us to keep it away from the waves, while he went to rescue the rafters.

The search found Ann dead, and one woman with broken rib, and the rest unharmed but traumatized. Our tears were uncontrollable.

That night there was a meeting about whether we should continue our journey. We held hands and the Peruvian tour leader communicated with spirits who told him, "Yes. That's what Ann wants." Her friend seconded. Everybody obliged with a broken spirit. An inquiry was started by the Peruvian government as they care about tourism and see cocaine as the single factor causing impaired judgment in raft leaders, a serious crime there.

The Pacific-powered currents claimed Ann's life, no doubt about it. Our German tour guide never explained why he deprived himself of such an exciting opportunity.

And I was hit by a bug or altitude sickness or the tragedy of the loss and felt sick as a dog all night.

LOST IN THE CORNFIELDS OF PERU: THE PRINCE ON A DARK HORSE

After a tough day, losing one of our travel mates to raging waves, another to hospital with injury, and three deciding to return, and a tougher night with no stops to visit the bathroom, feeling lifeless, I joined our group on the bus leaving Lima in the morning.

I was quite out of it. Dehydration, continued nausea, abdominal cramps, and the sadness engendered by tragedy, all had taken the life out of me. I did not know I'd be much worse for days to come. Just wanted to overcome the foggy state of being there and yet not being there, and the extreme sense of weakness. We were going for another tourist attraction before embarking on our hike up the mountain for seven days.

After an hour or so, the bus stopped on a dirt road where multiple buses had arrived to deposit troves of tourists.

I came out of the bus and lamely followed the group, head down, my face scowled by malaise, and with a stooped posture. Every few seconds I'd look up to make sure I was following our group, now only ten of us, among the long lines of other tour groups all going to the same destination. I had little face recognition of our group members.

It was too early, there'd been too little personal contact, and I was too agonized to socialize.

Within a few minutes (and God knows if it was just a few minutes considering my mental fog), I saw myself alone on the edge of a cornfield branching out to multileveled endless adjacent cornfields going timelessly into the horizon. It was a beautiful, sunny horizon, perfumed by fresh air and row upon row of baby corn. All lost to me. There was no trace of humans. No trace of human talk, whispers, distant din.

At first, I tried to retrace my steps and go back, but I realized that my feet—usually equipped with some sense of a map—could not help me. Back and forth, I was going deeper into the cornfields.

Then my lifelessness was replaced by an alarmed state and I was suddenly worried about being found by the wrong person. Nausea and abdominal pain in the background, my mind was seeing my imminent death as clearly as the crisp morning and seamless blue sky. A Canadian passport, I was told, was very precious. It was my understanding that many drug offenders under unwavering death penalties were looking to escape Peru. I imagined thieves stealing my passport and then letting me go. The penalty for harming tourists, was too high if they got caught—tourism is a major source of revenue for the Peruvian government after the cocaine trade.

I noticed a woman farmer not too far away from me, her skin darkened and translucent by the caressing sun, her build as small as a prepubescent child, dressed in national farmer batik with black and dark red stripes. I approached and said hello and mumbled and mimed "Tourist!—*really? She did not know!*—Which direction?" She looked at me intensely with kind eyes and waved in no clear direction. She was telling me she did not understand. I put some Spanish twist in my next inquiry. No help. She was a genuine Peruvian with her native tongue firmly in place. I ran back. Where did I get that energy? I was really dying and now I was terrified of being killed.

I met a few more farmers—some waved their hands in a particular direction that I followed only to find myself deeper in the lower terrace of these maze-like interconnected maize fields. Then, suddenly, I heard my name softly coming from some randomly placed trees. And I announced my existence with a loud "Yes!"

Within a few seconds, a bejewelled prince on a regal white Arabian horse, disguised as a slightly built, young, dark-featured man with a farmer's hat on a small, dark-brown mule appeared. A Peruvian tracer had been dispatched who found me in no time.

Ah, the relief I felt of no longer contemplating my violent death in the hands of innocent passport thieves was impossible to describe. In no time my lifelessness and symptoms came fiercely back.

The smiling young man descended and politely lifted me onto the mule. No words were exchanged. He knew my state better than me. And my immense appreciation.

In a few minutes I was back to the dirt road where my traumatized travel mates were going to throw all their pent-up dark emotions on me.

Of course, they were happy to see me alive. Nobody could have gone through another violent loss. But nobody hesitated to express the frustration I had caused because of my "wandering"!

The Peruvian guide invited the horseman, the tour operator, and ten of us to make a circle holding hands and to sit on the dirt road. Everybody was given a chance to trash me with polite words.

The question was whether I should be eliminated from the tour and sent back to Toronto. There was a chorus of "Yes! Yes!" I started to fantasize the relief of going back and feeling sick in my own bed in Toronto. I said to the group that it was the right decision. In my state I couldn't possibly hike up the vertical mountains for seven days.

Two people started to cry. They said they couldn't fathom losing another one.

There was a lawyer in our group who, for some reason, had a favourable view of me. He was adamantly against my exit. The Peruvian leader said as we could not make a unanimous decision, he would contact spirits—the same spirits he had approached the day before regarding the continuation of our tour after losing Ann.

In silence, we witnessed him communicating with the spirits in a way about which we had no clue. After about a minute's negotiation, he looked at me with a smile and said, "Spirits advised that you stay!"

Except for a woman in her early fifties—a social worker who had a firm belief that I had abused tranquilizers and that's why I had wandered off, or else that dementia had set in—the rest of the group had a sense of relief. This same woman was one of the five people who'd completed the hike and never stopped asking me intricate questions about her relationships or anything that came into her mind. She never acknowledged my sickness. And I stayed sick. So sick that, though I stubbornly kept walking, on two occasions when dusk was approaching, they forced me to ride on a little horse being led by a local horseman. I could not convince them that I had no power to hold onto the bridle, and there was no belt to harness me. I saw my death just a fall away. But I would not blame them as I did not want to hold the group hostage to my dismal speed. The lawyer who also finished the hike and the guide stayed kind to me all the way.

Madness of Love in India

I will go to India again, but next time I won't visit Taj Mahal. It should be on everybody's bucket list along with myriad other beautiful things on Earth.

I saw Taj Mahal a few years ago.

My nannies' stories indicated that the king of India, Shah Jahan fell in love with a Persian beauty called Momtaz and gave her all he could, including a palace made of the whitest marble adorned with precious stones, for which he hired a Persian architect. Once finished, it was so perfect that it was made clear that the architect had not revealed the design to anybody, and the king threw him down from a gigantic brick scaffolding built to construct Taj Mahal, at once. He did not want it to be replicated. Even a child could smell madness in the king, even if in a fictional story.

In India the story transformed but the king and his madness became real.

Taj Mahal is not a palace. It's a Tomb, a gravesite, a mausoleum in honour of Momtaz, the Persian wife of Shah Jahan, Turco-Mongol King of India, descendant of Genghis Khan and Timur the Lame. Mongols made the largest land empire from twelfth century through seventeenth century They were ruthless, artistic and great war tacticians.

The teenaged Mongol Prince fell in love with a girl his own age, they married and she bore him twelve—in some versions, twenty-eight—children. She died in her last delivery. By that time her husband was the king and he spent the next twenty years completing the monument and its courtyard gardens. The king was so obsessed with making a masterpiece defined by symmetry, the essential feature for aesthetics of architectural art for that time, that he completely gave up governing and all other aspects of life.

Shortly after Taj Mahal, was complete, his son, perceiving him to be mad, put him in house arrest. He died two years later. He was buried beside his wife. Some romantics think the vacant land at the other side of Yamuna River was planned for a black Taj Mahal, the king's tomb.

From the marble gateway, almost a half kilometre walk from the monument, there are two parallel paths winging a long pool straight to the mausoleum. It was late in the morning with the sun boasting its gold in a pale turquoise sky with no clouds, when I looked at the mosque-like white monument. It looked like it was made of one piece of marble with a halo around its dome—a halo with the word "love" engraved on it.

There was no halo and no engraved "love" on it, just an impression in my mind.

Years ago, when visiting Egypt, I kept having a similar impression. Then the word "eternity" kept being etched on all the pyramids and inner cities. It felt like life as it is had no meaning but being a passage through which we had to bribe our way with offerings to those with power on Earth, like kings and religious leaders, to avoid dire punishments in eternity.

A few years later, I will have the impression of the word "creation" on volcanic mountains and caves in the Galápagos Islands.

I closed my eyes and opened them and looked again. The halo and "love" appeared for a split second, and then they were gone. I was wondering if this, the "love" impression was what brought throngs of tourists here. All the painstaking labour and hard work of artisans, architects, and artists, to express the pain a man suffered for losing his wife should have left some long-lasting trace in the surrounding air.

Taj Mahal (Place for Crown) is built at a river bank, Yamuna River. Could the halo I saw be the haze formed by evaporated water? And the rest by my imagination?

Taj Mahal looked as perfect as its miniature plastic and clay artifacts that are sold on the streets. Its legendary inlaid precious stones have all been looted and some of its marble has been defaced and it suffered some decay in the past. But it's looked after now. Upon entering the essence of perfection and symmetry, there is a sense of disappointment; it's just a gravesite. The replica of Momtaz's grave is at the centre, and beside it is a smaller one for Shah Jahan (the real graves are in the basement.) I just thought the symmetry he worked so hard for was dented by his own grave. Maybe that's the essence of love: Perfect reciprocation is hoped for but each one gives a bit more.

BRUSHES WITH DEATH: DOUBLE IN RAAMSAR

Oral Persian stories begin with: One was there. One was not there. Beneath the cerulean Dome, there was a …

I consider myself to be very cautious bordering on fearful, and some people think the same about me. But here and there I am addressed as adventurous and I don't like it. My footprint, alas, shows I have lived adventurously. Indeed, I've had brushes with death from early on. None has been a conscious decision by me. It looks like I have a double who is there when I am not.

In the height of what was called the "White Revolution" in Iran, Shah and Farah were making genuine efforts to connect with their nation. As if for the first time he had decided to make Iran his home now that he had an heir or two. One small way was to invite school and university girls with top marks in Tehran to come for two weeks, to a well-organized camp near his summer palace and to invite them for an afternoon tea, not a high tea, at his palace.

The camp was located in one of the most beautiful northern seaside towns of Iran called Raamsar, a resort where the rich, turquoise blue of the Caspian Sea was crowned by dark emerald green forest on the central Alborz mountains, and the golden sun had solitary reign in the sky unhampered by silvery celestial lakes. And at night the cerulean sky was generously splashed by millions of winking stars, while the moon kept changing its location and size. I was in this camp in Grade 10, and in the first year of university. It was so different when we went to Raamsar as a family, when we would freely roll on the sand and fearlessly play with the waves.

In camp every day we were given marks for the neatness of our tent while we were participating in a disciplined schedule: breakfast, mountain climbing, art lessons, swimming in the Caspian at our leisure, lunch, rest, preparation for a performance in the evening, dinner and bed. The fresh food was made by expert chefs on the premises.

Early in the morning, a group of over forty girls with an experienced camp leader would start to climb the densely forested Alborz. We would follow closely as it was a path least travelled. At my second time in the camp, on the third day of climb, a few of us lost track of our leader. There were five or six of us, all in our late teens, from various faculties. Some started to cry. For some reason, I, who had no experience on forested mountains but had climbed other mountains numerous times with my family as a child, reassured everyone that I would find the way. They were like little trusting babies and wanted to hold onto me so this time around they wouldn't get lost. But I set a law: they must not take one step forward until I declared it safe ground. All around us looked like one green treed precipice after another. One step more and we would be into the air.

Then I detected a flat green space not bigger than a square metre just half a metre below the surface we were on. I called the girls and showed it to them and instructed them to stay where they were until I descended and knew it was safe. Then I held a strong branch of the tree near me and dropped myself to the flat, green surface. My feet did not touch the ground and I felt like I was floating in the air by high-speed gravity only to be slowed by protruding branches of the forest and raspberry bushes. I opened my eyes and saw I was descending parallel to the mountain and saw my death. I felt very sad for my parents and ashamed to have caused such a loss for them. I was also hearing the scream of the girls halted by panic saying, "Toghra fell."

After the exhilarating last smooth part of this unwanted ride, I fell down and remained completely intact, save some massive skin bleeding caused by raspberry bushes, on the campground right in front of the doctor's makeshift office. Some students were doing voluntary work there.

The sound of my fall called them out of the tent. They started to laugh, saying, "Doctor, she has smeared raspberries on her skin!" My non-smiling face sobered them and everyone started to pull the thorns out of my skin and bandage my hands and legs.

The screams of my lost fellows had saved them as they were soon located by the leader. I was told to stay in my tent so the girls didn't get scared by the (sorry) sight of me and refuse to climb. And I had to wear long pants and sleeves at dinnertime.

The leader was right to be angry with me. The safest way was to scream and cry loudly. That's so true in life when we have come up short of options.

In the designated afternoon to visit the palace, we were each served one cup of tea with accompanying sugar cubes by elegant servants without Shah and Farah. The tea was served in the best bone China, humbled by the beauty and delicacy of a solitary intact tea leaf the size of a brown sequin gently floating at the bottom of the golden-brown tea. I had never seen one. And I have not seen it again. It was Lahijan tea, grown in the eponymous town, very close to the camp's location. The majority of people only got broken large leaves.

My other brushes with death will come later in more violent forms and with my increased wisdom and caution, as if my double keeps being there when I am not.

CIVILIZATION AND ATROCITY

The cruise to Alaska was the last one of the season. It would be too cold after September for people like me, whose idea of travelling is always to go to a warm place. It included a number of expeditions and minor hiking: all cold, a bit icy, and rainy.

We would leave the ship on a daily basis and, within walking distance, get into vans designated for different excursions.

One early morning we arrived at a van with no driver/tour guide there to greet us.

After half an hour, a young woman, looking unkempt and out of sorts, and dressed in pyjamas, with flowing, uncombed hair, appeared, walking in a rush. The dreadful thought in my mind was that she had partied the previous night and was under the influence of marijuana.

By that time, the epidemics of cannabis from the early seventies had subsided, but I had become well versed in seeing its effects and after-effects of ensuing a severe mental imbalance.

During the epidemics, marijuana had taken over North America as a pretender to bring peace to the world. It was a post-Vietnam War phenomenon. The peace sign, a V formed with the first two fingers parting while the rest made a fist, was expressed by people who had been called hippies in the late sixties and early seventies. They were dressed in printed, flowery pattern cotton from India, mostly barefoot, with headbands tightened over long, unmanaged hair—women and bearded men, wearing multiple beady necklaces and bracelets. They looked STONED. But even a double take could elicit a violent response ranging from an aggressive stare or verbal profanity to an actual physical outburst.

In Toronto, there was such an infiltration pretty much all over but the density was far more around the Yorkville and Kensington Market areas, where men and women in their early twenties, holding hands, were squatting on the streets or stretching their legs, leaning on the walls. The pungent odour was common on the streets and in the movie houses. Marijuana was considered a new discovery in a new world, not an old drug with considerable destructive power.

In a way exactly like today! Except that now it has numerous imaginary medicinal powers, too.

We had heavy academic and clinical loads as residents. We were isolated from the real world and barricaded inside the hospital. Particularly late at night, we were seeing and touching real casualties among the stoned. Usually, police brought a totally out-of-order loud, rambling person who was resisting help by attacking the helper. They were always admitted, tranquillized overnight, and, by morning, sheepish but restless and insisting on going. Not repenting or regretful. Cannabis, weed, herb, is scarier for me than alcohol. The drunkard is so easy to detect but with cannabis, the storm is masked by a passive surface. And cognitive impairment lingers much longer.

So, I was terrified being driven by our hippy, (though hippies had long disappeared) possibly-under-the-influence-of-weed driver. I had every intention of asking her to drop me off at any point on the road if I suspected impairment.

As soon as we sat in the van and she started to drive, she apologized sincerely for being late, choking a little with every pronounced word. She was far from being under any influence. Indeed, she was too sober.

She went on: They set fire in my place last night. I had to run at the middle of the night to my landlord's place. That's why I am in my pyjamas and my hair is such a mess. Her unbrushed, long, wavy, light-brown hair had the glint of at least $200 worth of colouring. She was far from an aged hippy.

As she was driving along a strip of water with an inlet of land, she pointed with her right hand "That's where I live," she said. "I mean, I lived." It was a small cabin in the middle of some shrubbery that was turning brown.

She said the land lord had a few of them, including his own house, on this little piece of land that was not quite an island. Only a cabin with a bathroom. It was the cheapest she could get as her work was seasonal. After this cruise, she would be going to Florida as a tour guide.

The government had sent the owner a few notices that he should evacuate as they wanted to turn the land into a park. But he knew that they could not force him to give up his place and source of livelihood. They had threatened him that they had to do something he may not like. So, the night before had been their first show of their might. She had woken up to the smell of smoke and noticed flames raging outside and had run out to her landlord's place. They'd had to report it to the police.

As she got more relaxed she revealed herself to be a very pleasant and informed tour guide. She told us that she was of French-Canadian descent from parents who had settled in Alaska years before.

The memory of a story an Anglophone French-Canadian had told me about her parents' house in Gaspé, Québec, during the seventies, came to life. Generations of fishermen with French and English backgrounds had lived there for over a hundred years. The government had decided to turn this extraordinary piece of land and water into a provincial park. Initially the government offered the Gaspe homeowners good prices for their dilapidated houses, but a few who sold, regretted it. The money was worth nothing in the city and also, they were fishermen and could not make a living anywhere but at the seaside.

Some of the villagers refused to cooperate and were informed that their houses may randomly be set on fire. And they were. Always in the middle of the night. For some time, French- and English-speaking neighbours suspected each other, but then they realized the government was doing what it had declared it would and, one by one, people left. The person who told me this sad tale was a little girl when her parents migrated to Montreal and had to live on welfare. She finished high school and became a secretary.

A few years later, I read in a newspaper that the government had acknowledged the unfair aggravation it had caused for Gaspé's fishermen forty years ago. By chance I met the lady, who was happy with the government's official apology, again. As a consolation, the surviving children were given one free pass to the beautiful Gaspésie National Park!

Roman emperor Nero burnt Rome over 2,000 years ago. People had disagreed with his plan to modernize Rome because there was no provision for the majority, who were going to lose their humble dwellings. Apparently, he played violin when Rome was being burned.

GIFTS FROM A FRIEND

Zohreh is a friend with a contagious joie de vivre. She is smart and energetic and has lived life to the fullest. Her company is not only energizing but inadvertently informative.

Once she went for Haj to Mecca as a truly secular Moslem—more just to be spiritual.

As a curious, inquisitive engineer, she found out that the famous black stone set into the eastern corner of the Kaaba, the ancient building in the centre of the Grand Mosque in Mecca, Saudi Arabia, is solid quartz. Kaaba is the original hut of worship built by Prophet Abraham, now rebuilt as a stone edifice in the shape of a thirteen-metre-high cube. She said that there is a sense of total psychological and spiritual alignment if one gets close to it. She was wondering if the attraction toward this black stone was based on the physicochemical properties of quartz, which give this sense of alignment.

In her passionate way, Zohreh recounted the story of how Abraham's wife, Sara, unable to bear a child, instructed him to take her young maid, Hajar, as a concubine, and Esmaeel was born. Esmaeel soon was brothered by Isaac, who was born unexpectedly from Sara. For some mad reason, good Prophet Abraham sent Hajar and little Esmaeel (I am using Farsi pronunciation) to the wild to dispose of them. But resourceful, thirsty Hajar in the barren Saudi land found a spring and not only quenched her own thirst and that of Esmaeel, but made a business by selling the water to caravans with parched passengers.

In harmony with Zohreh's sense of humour, I thought, she told me that, when Abraham heard of Hajar's survival and lucrative business, he travelled all the way from Iraq and claimed his paternity over Esmaeel. He made Hajar's hut into a house of worship, even a more lucrative business. Noble Isaac became father of future Jews, and left-to-die Esmaeel became the father of future Moslems (I am using Farsi pronunciation).

Her sweet story was far more heart-capturing than the biblical one. I was determined to go and see Hajar's renovated hut, adjacent to Zamzam Well, mentioned in biblical stories as the freshest water on earth. Not being a devout Moslem, I opted out for the small Haj.

To go to Mecca, women should be accompanied by their husbands or a male relative, or they can become nominally a concubine of the tour leader or an eligible male. My son Neil expressed his interest in accompanying me. He is spiritual with no religious denomination. He googled all the information about Haj, and prayers, and became an ace pilgrim in the eyes of our pious group members.

Madineh had ultra-modern automatic umbrellas in the courtyard of a grand mosque, which open up in daylight and close at dusk. Its outdoor bazaars get closed for prayers while the streets get washed. It's a place one should buy fancy fresh dates with great caution. They may be rotten.

People stop and prostrate for prayers on the ultra-clean streets when Azan is heard from minarets of the Mosques. I did it many times and in a few minutes rows of people would get formed around me. It gives an indescribable sense of connection to humanity. And amazingly bestows gender equality. I as a woman with Hejab stay anywhere and start to say prayers and a number of people men and women stay behind me and around me and synchronize themselves with my motion!

In Mecca, our opulent hotel, adorned with gold and marble, was adjacent to Grand Mosque, the location of the Kaaba. Just a few steps along the marble pavement and we would be in courtyard of the Mosque: made clean and shiny by the non-stop cleaners around. This courtyard sees thousands of pilgrims of all ages and walks of life from all over the world simultaneously walking in the most disciplined way around and around the Kaaba, saying prayers and meditating. But there is not the slightest possibility of body contact, despite the density of the pilgrims.

Zamzam Well, covered with hilly marble, is in front of the Kaaba and accessible by multiple tabs for pilgrims to take it as a souvenir. I drank Zamzam water and looked at shiny black stone from a close distance. I hoped I felt aligned.

At lunchtime, my tour mates said touching the black stone was essential to our pilgrimage, so I walked back to the courtyard of the Grand Mosque and noticed how impossible it was to find an opening to cross at least twenty meters of solid flesh to reach the stone building, never mind the black stone. And then, lo and behold, I found opening after opening until I reached the black stone and touched it with the tip of my fingers as pilgrims had high speed in that area. Everybody wanted to touch the sacred stone.

I returned to my group victoriously—only to feel defeated again. I should have put my face inside the stone, where millions of pilgrims, after nearly 1,400 years, had created a head-sized space.

I had asked Neil to come with me now that I knew how openings got formed by higher power if we were really determined to reach our goals. After a while, Neil declined as he felt an obsession with touching the stone versus simply walking would rob him of the spirituality of the experience. I headed alone and, again, opening after opening appeared and, in no time, I was facing the sacred stone with a space carved in it by the sobbing faces of pilgrims over thirteen centuries. I placed my face in it and realized I could stay there as long as I wanted; the pilgrims were truly obliging. But I relented soon and felt drenched with a sense of shame when I detected a sobbing man, his face and palms attached to the wall.

His very rough skin and clothes gave him the look of a Turkish farmer. I thought he did not know how close he was to the sacred stone. I felt compelled to do a good deed as dictated by my Zoroastrian DNA. The three principles of Zoroastrian ethics are: think well, talk well, and act well. I had to bypass talking. I just took the man's rough right hand forcefully and made it touch the sacred stone. He did not look at me and resisted my unwanted good deed vehemently.

After I turned back to continue the pilgrimage around the Kaaba, my left shoulder was suddenly squeezed with such a force I thought it would break. It was just for a few seconds. And it took just a few seconds for me to realize that I had touched the man's bare hand with my bare hand. All his prayers had gone to waste. Fair punishment.

All my psychological and spiritual alignment became null.

Away from Mecca, westward, we visited the modern ancient seaside city of Jeddah, which means "female ancestor," where the gravesite of Eve is preserved. Women in Saudi Arabia cannot go to any cemetery, not even to pay respect to Eve.

We walked along the Red Sea and, surprisingly, all along the seashore we saw large abstract sculptures. Some concrete interpretation has asserted that arts in the form of sculpture and painting are forbidden in Islam (Eslam). I thought: but this climate breeds art. So, could it be that at its height of artistry, the creation of *objets d'art* in human form became so fascinating that it gave the impression of idolatry? And the destruction of all the art by a surge of spirituality of the time turned the art to history. Now the artists in Jeddah were springing back but were careful not to create the human figure.

I thanked Zohreh for my trip to Mecca. While visiting her in Finger Lakes, she suggested I see the Tree of Forty Fruits at nearby Syracuse University.

I did, after saying farewell to her and her husband. Syracuse University looked like a modern temple and, somewhere in its sprawling, beautifully designed roads to various faculties, there was a tree not bigger than a peach tree, bearing forty fruits. I just trusted Zohreh, and the inscription under the tree as summer had far gone.

Some people keep giving gifts.

ALL PERILS ARE IN OUR EYES: IN PRAISE OF GOOD MOVIES

I read *The Iliad* and *The Odyssey* shortly after Neil was born. Pregnant with his little brother, I had severe insomnia. The best relief was tasting the rich collection of books my husband had accumulated, reading many of them cover to cover. I focused on the meaning, not the story. I did not recall my reading, until years later when I travelled to Turkey and visited the site of the attack by the Greeks on Troy, and saw a replica of the Trojan horse. It was then that Homer came to life for me.

A short while ago, Neil sent me a mini-series made for TV, from 1968 and titled *Odysseus*. He praised the producer for his painstaking work. I was smitten by the story! Although blind, Homer had made such a splendid visual rendition of the story and its beautiful allegory, but my wrong focus had taken me astray. This miniseries brought *The Odyssey*, and the travails and perilous journey of Odysseus, much closer to my mind.

The blind poet born in Turkey many thousands of years ago, like all poets, is immortal—not just because of his voluminous intriguing and enthralling tales about the life-endangering journey of a cunning champ, but because he offers us universal truth. The essence of our life as humans contains contrasts, controversies, and paradoxes. Odysseus could be any one of us. Opposites, side by side. And to the extreme. Caught in the interplay of fate and free will, integrity and immediate gratification, a self-serving tendency and concern for others.

Poets, like nature, offer us a map so we can navigate and carve our own unique, straight and narrow paths. Straight and narrow have been known, from time immemorial, as the surest way toward personal happiness. The only worthwhile goal where there is no chance of wavering, except activating and enhancing our own potentials. In Shakespeare's words, "The eye does not see itself. But by reflection, by some other things."

We cannot see our own face, but we can touch it. Or maybe Homer, our Turkish poet, had said it in a different word arrangement. Therefore, we need a mirror – whether through nature, or via man-made ones in the form of stories.

If the search is in vain, then we get drowned by the perception of our God-like beauty, like our mythical brother Narcissus, whose death by drowning in a sparkling spring that reflected his beauty, gave birth to an eponymous delicate, fragrant flower. If lucky, while meandering in the intricate mingling of the good and bad of our nature, we can carve a way, always respecting our free will while accepting fate.

Homer's epic tale of Odysseus starts with Iliad, a series of disastrous events in search of single goal of victory. Greeks attacking Turks (Trojans) to get their honour back. Helen, a Greek married woman, next to Aphrodite in beauty, was given in an intrigue as a trophy to a Trojan prince. They got her back.

The whole fiasco started with an apple! Just like in Biblical story. what's about apples?

The Goddess of Discord was not invited to one of Zeus's lavish parties, and she had to heal her wound by plotting revenge. "If I am not included, then nobody will have fun." But if she *were* included, nobody would have had fun—except herself, by feeding discord in others. Standing outside the walls of the palace, she threw an apple into the giddy partygoers. On it was inscribed: "Must be eaten by the most beautiful woman."

Now everybody knew Aphrodite to be the goddess of beauty. But everybody knew also that Hera, the wife of Zeus, the god of gods, in today's language, came from the most powerful and hideous family, was well past her prime, and had to always be considered the best of all. And Athena the Goddess of Competition and Revenge had to be considered, too. A tricky courtier chose the naive Paris, a Turkish prince, to judge who was fairest of all. Paris was aware of the old lady's legendary jealousy and was silent, until Aphrodite promised him the most beautiful woman in Greece, Helen, should he dare to speak truth. Paris made the fatal judgment.

Let me digress for a moment. Why does the apple have such power in human destiny? We were kicked out of heaven because of it, only to return with conditions. Over 10,000 years ago, according to Greek mythology, it started twenty years of bloodshed and human misery and eventually return to hope. And in the nineteenth-century children's story, "Snow White," the jealous queen tricks Snow White into eating a poisonous apple. Her mirror on the wall kept telling her Snow White was fairest of them all.

Back to *The Iliad*.

Hera had to protect her dignity by summoning all champions to go after Paris and follow him to Troy. The top champion was tricky Odysseus, who tried to be exempted by mimicking mental illness. He put his newborn son in front of a plow pulled by a donkey and an ox, to prove his insanity, but it did not work.

The Iliad tells the story of the Greeks taking nine years to reach Troy and one year to win Helen, and counts up the champions and young men from both sides who lose their lives in the fighting.

The Odyssey is the tale of return of Odysseus to his wife Penelope. Ten years of his personal journey back to Ithaca, feeling trapped by Athena, the goddess of revenge and art and competition, in alliance with the god of the oceans, Poseidon. They were working against him by making the sea stormy. Or so Odysseus thought. But one nymph, Calypso, with whom Odysseus had a good seven years' blissful cohabitation in a remote Greek island, noticed his sadness. Or maybe he was bored by that time. She told him that he could go back to his wife anytime he wanted. Odysseus told her that she, empowered by Athena, has made the sea so stormy there was no chance for him to leave.

Calypso then corrected him: "Odysseus, the perils are all in your eyes. Look at the see. It's calm." When Odysseus threw a hopeless glance toward the Mediterranean Sea, he noticed the calm azure and enough boards and logs to make a raft. Athena had become supporter of Odysseus!

Calypso wakes us up. There is much we may consider entrapment by nature, gods, God, fate, maybe even our own inner barriers.

Praise to good movies.

THE RADIANCE OF YOUTH IS A CAUSE FOR CELEBRATION

I read with disbelief Ms. C. opining on the inappropriateness of women anchors wearing sleeveless clothes or showing bare skin while on the job. Ms. C. is an accomplished lawyer and academic who also managed to be elected prime minister of Canada in 1993. It was a significant victory, even if it lasted only five months.

About that time, a widely published photo appeared, where a bare-shouldered Ms. C. held her black legal robes on a hanger, concealing what was implied to be her nude body. It was quite innovative at the time to depict the suggestive erotic beauty of a woman side by side with her intellectual prowess.

Ms. C. spend a good part of her youth living with an older man almost her father's age. Later, for a few years, she lived with a Russian man. In the last twenty years, she has been married to a man nearly twenty years her junior. It's amazing how this person, who has thoroughly enjoyed an expression of personal liberty, now in her seventies, is feeling threatened by other women in their prime of life.

It reminds me of an incident a few years ago when I was visiting Iran. I repeatedly heard how women in Iran had lost their sense of morality, and were engaged in the most disreputable actions and choices – culminating in the sex trade. The words were harsh, and I personally felt sad about all this.

But despite the reported epidemic proportions of such a horrible social phenomenon, I could not identify any such despicable specimens of femininity during my long walks on major streets. I had imagined herds of women standing on the streets, covered from head to toe, offering their wares. Not like the orderly, glass-walled boutique cages displaying tame nude sex merchants in Amsterdam, or a solitary naked woman dancing and waving from the window of a special restaurant in New Orleans' red-light district. And then, one day during an outing with an old relative, she pointed to the other side of the street and whispered: "God forbid! Look at those street women! Look how openly they are soliciting men!"

I looked up with interest. Finally, I was going to see these aggressive sex traders clad in hijab.

What I saw was a group of young women in their late teens or early twenties radiating with the beauty of youth, covered head to toe, with artfully displayed make-up, stylish outfits that were in defiance of oppression and forced head coverings. They were colourful as a bouquet of fragrant flowers, and were laughing and engaged in conversation. And they were oblivious to the world around them, men and women.

The offender seemed to be my relative. Having passed her prime, all aesthetic curves turned to unmanageable lumps, with no effort for personal improvement, and maybe no hope. And no connection to her own youth. Did she not remember herself through them? A free-spirited giddy young girl enjoying personal liberties during Shah's reign that, for these young women, would have sounded like myths?

Did she only focus on her physical beauty and miss all opportunities for personal development?

Enjoying youth and indeed any stage of life is a personal responsibility. Isn't life all that we have?

Wouldn't Ms. C. consider her life a series of accomplishments, culminating in being loved by a husband twenty years younger than herself? In that case, the bare skin of young women would only activate remembrance of the beauty of her own youth and how she shared it with the world around her and called it a "work of art."

Let us celebrate the universal works of art that we encounter throughout our lives, including the transient radiance of youth.

BROTHERLY LOVE: WHO BENEFITS FROM POLITICAL STORMS?

In the advent of another political tsunami in Palestine, I reflected on my personal experience in two journeys. Why on earth was everybody trying to crack a perfectly OK egg?

India is so rich in civilization, history, geography, and actual wealth and poverty, that even those born there can never claim to have seen it all. Contradictions are natural features in all ancient cultures. In life, too.

One site we visited was the Ganges River at the location where the traditional cremation of Hindus, the bulk of India's population, takes place. The dead are brought to the edge of the Ganges in the humblest fashion on a wooden cot. There it's washed, sprinkled with a mound of marigold petals and ointment. Then some scented candles will be lit around the corpse surrounded by firewood, set on fire and released into Ganges water.

While currents take the body to the stream, mourners recite prayers.

Right before we entered the river bank, the town looked like other populated areas in India: busy, crowded, suffused with the tempting aroma of street food, and lively with Indian music and the hustle and bustle of daily business. There is also a distinct feature in this hub:

an increased density of Indian Moslems, easily distinguished by their clothing. Men wearing long white robes and a cap, women wearing loose, patterned pants and long tops, and a head cover. No sari showing the bare midriff. There is a butcher shop displaying carcasses of cows, lambs, goats, and, outside the store entrance, cages holding chickens, and piles of firewood.

This is an otherworldly experience. This Hindu nation that actually treats cows as sacred, the symbol of nurturance and giving, which is vegetarian to the bone, buys firewood for their dead from a Moslem who slaughters the cow.

The Moslem butcher with a religious conviction that forbids cremation provides firewood for his Hindu customer.

This brotherly love, absolute acceptance and respect for the others, despite irreconcilable differences, is what humanity is all about. And yet not too long ago a political tsunami forced the exodus of Moslems from India's mixed neighbourhoods, ripping the nation's organs apart, forming a makeshift country called Pakistan, which is now over seventy years old.

Palestine and Israel combined occupy such a small piece of earth, but are so interwoven through the millennia with internal contradictions that one wonders how they could ever be separated. It's not like the chicken-and-egg riddle. It's like, how could an egg be an egg without white or yellow?

I was hiking in Israel on a tour called "Jesus's Trail." The majority of my tour mates were secular Christian hikers. It was Passover and our hotel had stopped serving bread. Only unleavened bread was available, honouring the plight of Jews from Egypt in millennia past. President Obama was visiting Israel.

I was going to see the famous mosque at the centre of the ancient bazaar in Jerusalem. Every store was operated by either a Moslem or a Jew, and each was almost indistinguishable from the other. I was stopped at the entrance to the mosque by a group of soldiers who took me as an entertainment of the day and I played along. They wanted to be sure I was a real Moslem, and not carrying an explosive with me.

The Israeli soldiers scattered through Jerusalem are mostly eighteen-to-twenty-one-year-olds, carrying guns, and sometimes large rifles, which scared their gun-shy Canadian-born tour mates to death: "Oh, God, these kids are carrying guns." As for me, who was raised in a militarized environment, the scene was close to home except for the gun-saturated streets. The soldiers who were not carrying guns were Palestinians who had accepted Israel as the winner in current dispute. But except for this feature, they were indistinguishable.

Both groups, men and women, were voluntary-conscript high school graduates. They would be rewarded with tuition-free university education.

The aforementioned group surrounded me with impish grins, trying to look like serious officials. One who had no gun said, "Prove that you are a Moslem! Say something from the Quran. Knowing with 100 percent certainty that the young Moslem had little knowledge of the book, I recited a verse in my best Arabic. I had gotten entrance to a mosque in Malaysia, at the wrong time for prayers, with the same performance. It was absolutely impressive. He stopped me at the middle as if it was too much for him. Then one who was carrying a gun pointed at a bottle of olive oil I had purchased from a nearby Palestinian merchant and said with forged suspicion, "And what is that?" I said he could read it.

He said, "How do I know it's not explosive?" I said he could drink it! They put away their forged official look, and he said the bottle would be kept in his "uncle's store" and that I could get it after visiting the mosque.

When I went back to get my olive oil, I saw the soldier who had the gun in lively conversation with the store owner, having tea together. I asked him jokingly, "How come your uncle is a Moslem?"

Both said, "What's the difference? We are the same." I surely believed in their brotherly love.

Later in that hike I went to see Nazareth and it was darkened when I returned to Jerusalem. On my way to the hotel, I noticed a sign for a Jewish market. Ever curious, I entered. Some stores were still open. One was a Jewish bakery with loads of freshly baked bread; next to it, a Palestinian woman was making something like French pancakes.

I was a few minutes away from our hotel and noticed all the roads were blocked by soldiers. President Obama was having dinner at President Netanyahu's house, a five-minute walk from our hotel. The barricades were up for safety reasons. During my half-hour wait, I met a number of local people and lots of tourists, gathered for clearing. We were in an animated discussion, with soldiers asking tourists about where they were from. It was at once a miniature United Nations. I met a local Jewish lady who held my hand and, fearing I may get lost, insisted on walking me to my hotel after clearing. The Little Jerusalem had complicated streets. Her house was close by, and although in daylight I'd had no problem finding my way, I was most grateful for my Jewish sister's magnanimity.

Relying on the Kindness of Strangers: New Year's Eve in Umm Qais

The green-eyed, sun-wrinkled Bedouin looked a thousand years old. I thought he was the bus driver. He was sitting on the interior ledge of the window beside the driver's seat, facing me. His deeply grooved ebony skin looked like a picturesque windswept Sahara, with meticulously formed parallel low hills and valleys of grey sand, converging at one point. His chin was covered with a short beard. His teeth were in decay and some were missing. He was wearing a dusty robe and headdress.

His cautious eyes kept scanning me, the only passenger in the bus going from Umm Qais to Amman. The buses in Jordan were beaten and old looking, but they functioned well and followed the schedule on the dot. We had about twenty minutes.

I can recite some prayers—really, verses—from the Quran accurately and even sound like an erudite Arab. And I know a few Arabic words, but cannot put two together. The Bedouin and I, however, were trying to find a way to communicate.

I looked at the map and realized how close we were to Israel, Iraq, Syria, Lebanon, and Iran—really just a few hours of a bus ride and I could have seen historical treasures like the Tower of Babylon and intriguing cities of antiquity like Damascus, at one time the centre of enlightenment. Except for Israel and Iran, I had not seen those jewels of humanity's younger days. They were currently being destroyed, one after another, by political hurricanes and earthquakes.

I showed him the map and pointed to Iraq, miming a journey there. He mimed a definite "No." A few other adjacent countries got the same answer. The war was boiling at any second and I knew it. Then he said, "Coffee?" I had just been overwhelmed a short while before by the generosity of young students who wanted to invite me to celebrate New Year's Eve because I was away from home. And now this old man with a few precious dinars in his pocket wanted to buy me coffee. He had read my mind! He put his hand in his pocket and presented me with a thick wad of notes—as if to say, "Don't worry. Money is not a problem. I mimed that coffee, their very strong Turkish style, was not good for me. Soon, he left and came back with fresh mango juice. He refused my offer to pay. A real wordless conversation started between us. He sat next to me and clicked on his smartphone. There was a photo of a happily laughing woman in her early thirties with flowing, light brown hair, ivory skin, and green eyes. His wife. Her smooth white skin was courtesy of a hijab protecting her from the sun. And he showed me another photo of his two young children. I showed him photos of my children. It occurred to me that he could be much younger than me. No, he certainly was. The missing teeth added to his perceived age. He looked at me kindly and left.

The bus was getting filled up and the driver came in.

I went to the bus driver to pay the fare and he waved his hand without looking at me. I thought maybe I was not giving the right amount so I added to it. Then the driver started the bus, pointed outside where the Bedouin was talking with a few men, and spotting me from the corner of his eye, waved farewell. The driver had the order to drive me for free.

I listened all the way to lyric Bedouin music with tears of tenderness in my eyes. Later, I heard it many more times in taxis.

In my hotel, where the signs of the New Year were all over, remembering the enthusiasm and generosity of my Bedouin kin, I treated myself to room service: spaghetti and meatballs! It tasted like it had been made by a seasoned Italian housewife.

HEROES

The recent untimely death of Canadian singer Gord Downie brought a new surge of national consciousness regarding the abuse of Indigenous people in Canada. Gord Downie will be remembered not only for his music, but for his genuinely heroic effort to revive the case of a little boy who, like many other children, never stopped trying to run back home. Chanie Wenjack was a sickly boy who, like thousands of other First Nations children, was forcibly removed from his family at age eight or nine, under the sanctioned British law to "beat the Indian out of them" and put in a residential school 600 kilometres away.

His final attempt to run away in the dead of winter caused him death by hunger and cold at the age of twelve. His heroic death opened the floodgates to crimes committed by residential schools in Canada.

He died in 1966. In 1969, I came to Canada, a country in juxta-position with the violent, racist U.S., characterized as the epitome of a civil and humanitarian culture. Having come from an ancient part of the world, I felt this young nation to be like a six-month-old baby, so pure and full of potential. I was unaware of the crimes its parents had committed.

"Children must pay for the misdeeds of the parents," is not as harsh as it sounds. It's a way of personal or collective redemption from our own human darkness. A transition from invisible, wretched torment to blissful transparency. This happens only in the human world. Animals and plants just get replicated as they are created at the height of their completion.

I had the good luck to get a Korean novel called *A Hen Who Dreamed She Could Fly* from its esteemed translator, Ms. Chi-Young Kim. It's basically a tapestry of poignant, emotional experiences in an oppressed environment in images of trapped animals. A weasel does carnage with wounded, weak, trapped animals.

There is a scene in which the protagonist, a hen called Sprout, finally becomes aggressive when it comes to protecting her egg. It is in fact an egg she found, belonging to a duck. She knows the weasel has eaten the mother of her egg. She gets access to the weasel's newborn babies and threatens to squash them with its legs. The weasel gets hurt and says, "It's not fair. If I eat you it's because nature has made you my food. I eat you because I am hungry. You are killing my babies because you are angry and hostile." Sprout, who has chosen her name, liking the idea of being a symbol of hope and potential, does not harm the babies but manages to keep the weasel away with the help of the egg's father, a duck, until the egg is hatched. When a teenage duck finally soars into space, her dream comes true. Sprout is a hero, as is the male duck who protects her.

The immense responsibility of carrying the title of *human* is lost to us. We have to constantly remind ourselves how far we still have to go by being aware of our potential to harm. It's not only through our own actions, necessarily, but through seeing what our fellow humans have done.

Nelson Mandela spent eighteen years in jail just for saying Black people were as human as white people. He refused an invitation for revenge after he was freed.

Ray Charles, the blind American singer raised by a hero of a woman, a single mother, was told never to play crippled. He did not brand himself as a Black man and enraptured his nation that was governed by racism and segregation law well into the sixties, with his music. He did not go to bursting concert halls to sing as a protest against segregation. About that time, Martin Luther King Jr. lost his precious life, fighting segregation with his enlightening speeches.

There are far more unsung heroes like Chanie and Ray Charles compared with a few celebrity varieties. But what collectively we can do as ordinary humans without being heroic will have far reaching effect.

Canada still has not sorted out its parents' bad behaviour with First Nations. It's 150 years old formally, but a hundred years older before it registered its birth.

The Vatican forever has turned a blind eye to Roman Catholic priests who physically and sexually abused and murdered First Nations' children in Canada, and sexually abused boys in general, elsewhere.

The U.S., despite efforts to compensate for dissemination bordering on extermination of natives, still uses Indians, a misunderstanding of illiterate never wanting to learn lost in the sea Christopher Columbus. Canada too still has "Indian Affairs." Racism in the U.S. is like a chronic illness even though the silent majority have been recovering.

And many more atrocious acts of the past and present around us can be used as sobering features to clean up our own backyards as we humans will not be able to see ourselves without a mirror.

My six-month-old baby now is in its teens and is more actively making its future. I am now in my thousands years and intertwined with this teenager. It takes a long time to turn from a weasel to a sickly dreamer of a hen, and hopefully a duck with a minor capacity to soar.

Ruin after Victory: Reykjavík Trashed

Iceland embodies the word "magic," as my daughter Naseem has said. It's like Taj Mahal invoking the word "love." And the Galapagos Islands invoking "creation," or Egypt bringing "eternity" to mind.

Little Iceland is a hilly, green space, with vaporous geysers and volcanic mountains spread throughout. And when we were there towards the end of August, blue-purplish lupines all along the roads were dancing in tandem with a gentle breeze.

Iceland has made a vigorous campaign to use tourism as a major source of revenue. Any country doing that is smart. Amsterdam is selling cannabis in "coffee shops" that directly target hapless tourists and teenagers in search of a good cup of Dutch coffee, and boasting an ultra-orderly bazaar of prostitution where female prostitutes of all forms, shapes, and races in glass cubicles openly offer their wares along major arteries of that beautiful city. Major Irish cities welcome tourists and locals into public houses (pubs) to drink until the supply is finished. In Lourdes, France, by giving the possibility of daily miracle, they lure hopeful tourists to buy holy water and light candles, creating sizeable wealth. And so on.

In Iceland, a futuristic country despite its long, complex history, boasting of fueling itself through the cleanest form of energy, and having little tolerance for corruption, the number one factor for attracting tourists is impeccable service. Anything to make tourists safe and comfortable is utterly important for the country. The overpriced accommodation and food are worth the honest presentation and the promises that rarely fail. There is little or no possibility of "buyers beware." What is delivered is what is promised.

Iceland provides a convenient and punctual transportation service for all touristic points.

The cleanliness of the capital city of Reykjavík is exemplary. Only Australia can be considered as equally tourist-conscious in offering similar services, but Iceland is like a boutique for tourist friendliness in terms of superb service offered without the contrived Japanese courtesy mingled with arrogance. What Iceland is selling is viewing a magical land.

Of course, we go to Iceland to enjoy visually the erupting geysers swirling up from the ground like a belly dancer with such flexibility and versatility to make variety of shapes and collapsing softly before standing up again. And sometimes a few of them make a cluster, like a choreographed corps de ballet.

Locals reserve seating to watch one of over 300 active volcanoes, at the time of eruption, the way we buy tickets for ballet or opera.

Floating in crystal-clear, steaming hot springs in a natural setting for free, or a superbly constructed and equipped spa for a good price is unforgettable.

The order and law without any representation of police breathes safety in the air. In August, the sun does not seem to set, but stores close sharply at six pm.

Restaurants are mostly outfitted with modern, spartan decoration but are singularly focused on offering good food.

The city of Reykjavík is small and manageable by foot, with straight streets and structure.

There is a green hill right at the centre where touristic streets converge.

In 2016 when I was visiting, there was a football match between Iceland's team and that of another country. And the whole world seemed to be sitting on that green hill watching the match from a street screen with absolute reverence interrupted by occasional cheers.

Among my vast areas of ignorance, the world of sports ranks high. My ignorance in this field is only superseded by my lack of interest. And yet I decided to join the crowd on the green hill, which was so packed that the proverbial needle could not be thrown. But I just wanted to join and be part of this healthy, happy show of humanity. The gentle Icelandic and tourist groups opened the way for me, step by step, like the gentle crowds in Mecca who allowed me to reach the black stone.

Here, I found a central point surrounded by mostly young people who were sitting on the green grass, holding a bottle of beer or carrying up to a dozen. I just became one with the group without even knowing which team was ahead. And yet, at the end, the roar of unmatchable joy coming out of the crowd like evanescent steam from geysers made me happy. Iceland had won after many years of being eliminated. Everybody got up and went to street food vendors, pubs, restaurants, or, like me, straight to bed.

The next morning, I went for my walk before the shops were open. I had walked the city four times before, early in the morning, enjoying its crisp air and admiring its immaculate streets in the face of huge numbers of tourists.

But that morning as I was approaching the green hill, the whole city seemed to have been trashed. It was like an apocalypse in real life. Empty water and beer bottles, intact and broken, carpeted the sidewalks and streets, with used wrappings and discarded food everywhere. The whole area was trashed. But there was no sign of destruction or vandalism.

I thought: it's going to take forever to clean it all up.

It reminded me of the degeneration caused by an apparent victory in war. All civilization trashed by the victor.

But in Iceland not rushing to clean up had to do with allowing the memory of jubilation to linger longer. There was no actual destruction.

At that very time, a major government figure was imprisoned because of proven corruption.

HAVE WE REALLY LOST OUR TAILS AND EVOLVED—OR ONLY CONCEALED THEM?

The Persian language is rich in voluptuous nuances. Maybe it's the result of having survived centuries of being dominated by other cultures, and of nations conquering Iran. And also, an inherent inclination to aggressively incorporate other languages, only to refine and enhance their poetic power. The land of poetry has given birth to talents like Hafez and Molavi, who created masterpieces in poetry through a hybrid of their mother tongue, Farsi, and Arabic Qur'anic verses.

Ordinary spoken Farsi is rich in similes, metaphors, and analogy. I have been taken by expressions involving tails. "Don't step on my tail." "Don't step on their tail." "Watch! Her tail is too long!"

The "tail" expression is very old, and has survived the declaration of evolutionary theory that decrees humans are apes who lost their tails. It seems that most mammals have some kind of tail. Humans have only a tail bone.

The closest interpretation of the Persian tail in modern English is *ego*. "Leave your ego at the door." The ego is a relic of a now defunct psychoanalytic empire that helped advance our modern-day understanding of the mind, stirring it away from mystification and witchcraft. In psychoanalytic literature, the ego is synonymous with self, observant of reality, and a doer.

Ego in ordinary, everyday language, however, refers to our undeveloped narcissistic core, which is potentially negative, destructive, and maligned. But colloquial Persian and English share this identical expression: "Putting one's tail between one's legs and going away." In both languages, it means failed entitlement and an overt experience of shame.

In the Persian language, the tail is the allegory of concealed narcissism. We don't see it because we don't have a tail, but it designates a space that expands beyond our skin. The tail indicates the expansive boundary that commands the world to watch for our entitlement to perfection. The bigger our tail, the larger the circumference of which others have to beware, minding our sensitivity. And the less is our culpability for hurting others. The large tail does not recognize the tails of others.

In close relationships it leads to a relentless effort to control and exploit those around us. In larger scales, it appears as entitlement to dominate other nations and exhaust their resources, even if we have to annihilate them. It was a driving force in colonial times and long before that, and is a foreboding power in present brutal trade wars. In legal terms it's called hubris.

One woman talking about her most loving husband who was prone to episodes of rage said, "He keeps saying don't put your foot on my tail. But his tail is vastly spread and we practically can't move!"

My own concealed, widely spread tail has to be wrapped around, folded back over and over, time over time, when it's been injured by others stampeding over it. Contrary to the evolutionary theory, I will never lose it. It's here to stay. And to help me develop. Each hurt requires me to wrap my tail tenderly and rush toward the safety of isolation. But only moments of this imagined healing intervention cause a severe deficiency of oxygen of love and pain far more severe than the injuries of my tail.

After all, my tail is only an abstract part of me. Its injuries can be prevented and remedied by simple consideration that all around me have their own tails—that is, the same afflictions and vulnerabilities. But those who are not aware of their tails only have more conviction of their entitlement and the impulse to strike the perceived offender.

Understanding this notion has helped me to develop empathy and become more adept at being sensitive toward others rather than being "sensitive." And I am getting better at wrapping my tail, and at times putting it between my legs and going away, caressing it in private and letting the magic of time heal its injury. It never shrinks.

Learning from its injuries and that others have the same condition, and that the oxygen of love can be maintained and enhanced by simply wrapping my tail make me never want to lose it.

It is the most vulnerable part of me—that is, the most lovable part of me. It is also easier for me to accept that, inevitably, I am going to hurt others, despite my sincere good intentions, as the circumference of others' tails can never be clear to me. I just notice it when injury has already happened. I feel deeply for the person without incriminating myself.

Narcissism pays with a bit of effort.

MY INNER JELLYFISH
AND INWARD STING

I have a mean streak. Its magnitude has at times hurt me more than the one who has been the subject of my meanness.

My awareness of it has become sharper as the imperceptible weight of youth has lifted. I become aware of it only after the act of meanness has been committed.

Even seconds before that, it felt like I was defending myself. Like the self-defence of a jellyfish.

In the tourist markets in Athens, I would bargain over a thousand drachma for a little clay pot while my preteen children made pained faces and pulled my hands, pleading with me to stop. Stop bargaining over one cent! The dignified Greek merchant was thinking the same but was humouring me.

In Ixtapa, an oceanfront resort in Mexico, they were three newly minted teenagers and were able to reason with me: "Mom, you are bargaining over a few cents!"

What do you mean? I would respond. *I reduced the price by a thousand pesos*. And the little boys or girls carrying the handmade jewellery in their multiple pockets were looking silently at my exaggerated fervour to make a fair deal. Fair deal? It was my fool coming to full display.

My meanness is far more palpable when I am faced with others' kindness. The kindness of a stranger who disappears like the will-o'-the-wisp, leaving no chance for reciprocation.

These experiences, exposures to the simple, pure benevolence of the human soul, were clarion calls alarming me when I strayed from my desired destination in pursuit of internal refinement, while walking in the path of the youth.

In my second year of residency, when cannabis had become the rock-star pastime for young and old in Toronto, I was admitting lost souls afflicted by pot-induced psychosis, a few cases each night, brought by police to emergency. It was at the Clarke Institute of Psychiatry, presently known as the Centre for Addiction and Mental Health. One night when I responded to being dispatched, I noticed the lady dispatcher in her cubicle at her switchboard had some oval, lumpy thing from the plant family in her hand. As she was briefing me about a case in an accent I later learned to be Jamaican, she was slicing the dark green thing, letting a dizzyingly brilliant orange colour emerge. I asked her what it was. "It's a mango. The good ones are in Jamaica." She cut a thin slice and tentatively offered it to me on her little knife, not sure if I would like it. I grabbed it. Hundreds of mangos later, the delicious, tart sweetness of that slice has never been replicated. I did not see her again.

Two years later, at the end of my residency, still poor as a church mouse, I managed to save enough to go to Jamaica, invited by my friend Hyacinth, a fellow resident, to stay with her family for a week. Haya's parents had left China at a young age and made a prosperous business in Jamaica. They did not speak English but showered me with affection. Except for my utter pleasure at being the lucky recipient, there was no reciprocation.

Walking along a main street in Kingston lined with large hibiscus trees, I was in awe of how the tapestry of red, yellow, purple, and white flowers had carpeted the pavement. I also noticed little mangos dropped all over, too. I remembered the delicious taste and those thoughtful, deep, dark eyes.

Haya took me to various interesting places. On one occasion we were on the Atlantic coast viewing other islands on the horizon, where the emerald of the ocean merged with the turquoise of the sky. The midday golden sun gave a pleasant embrace. I spotted a patch of plant green some distance away in the vast, waveless emerald and threw myself into the warm invitation of the ocean against Haya's advice. I was confident that I could swim the distance. After a while I gleefully looked back and saw Haya and her two sisters waving at me to return. I heard their muffled voices, but soon I was too far to see them other than just moving spots.

I had reached the green patch when suddenly the front of my whole immersed body was pierced by a million needles. I pulled myself up to the green and saw blood all over me. I swam back for my dear life, pained to death by stingers. And not knowing what had happened to me. The closer I got to the shore the more frantic the motion of the hands. The voices were saying "It's dangerous! Jellyfish!"

Haya and her sisters pulled out the stingers of the non-killer Atlantic jellyfish one by one. The Gorgon Medusa with snakes coming from her scalp is far less mean compared to the gorgeous jellyfish, which seduces the uninitiated with an appearance that suggests a silky, smooth touch.

On the eve of my departure, a duck was slaughtered for a safe trip and a dinner party was arranged. At the entrance to the dining room I was greeted by an elegantly dressed tall lady who towered over my slight figure. She was wearing long white gloves. We shook hands. Her deep, dark brilliant eyes contained timeless stories of us, like we knew each other from the deepest past. She left after being introduced: the chef and culinary artist.

Among other culinary artworks, at the middle of the table was a ship larger than fifty centimetres in length and height, with lacework of masts and several sails, made by crystal-clear candy threads, woven by pipetted liquid candy by one hand and carved into intricate patterns by the swift motion of the other hand. Those precious gloved hands I had generically shaken.

My show of appreciation was to consume the gift, to eat it, wear it, display it, as it fit. I have yet to see a similar table or taste what I enjoyed that evening. Like the taste of a thin slice of mango in an emergency department.

It was my mean streak that enabled me to savagely destroy and consume the culinary artwork.

Does kindness activate our meanness?

Maybe for me it's the only way I could convert it to kindness. My inner jellyfish, by stinging me, is my clarion call.

A Letter to Neil, Copied to Roy and Naseem

We had our own short-lived heaven.

It was based on my pure, authentic, primitive maternal instinct. I wanted to prolong it eternally. But it had to evolve.

And your dear dad came to rescue. He had fully and silently endorsed my rapt attention and perpetual smothering. He was truly a generous soul. He gave what he had never received. He had experienced the naturally occurring neglect in a family in survival mode with seven years drought in Saskatchewan, hunger daily during his early years on earth.

And he wanted these children of whom he had never dared to dream to get all the love and attention. And the wife from the Third World was manna from heaven.

And then one historic day he intervened and my balloon was burst. You had turned three. Thank God, of course.

He in his own quiet but very firmly determined tone, said, "I read about a 'preschool' called Montessori. Have a look!" It was like the eleventh commandment! He had that power.

My world tore apart. The gust of alteration in my fantasy was ear-deafening and blinding, like a snowstorm in the Arctic. I cried. He got up and left—probably to wipe his own tears.

The next day I was at Montessori tearfully, and you were registered.

You notice his choice of word: "preschool" not "daycare." He knew no child of ours would ever go to daycare!!!

The next September on the first day of daycare after I dropped you, Roy cried and said, "I want to be with Neil!"

My balloon was burst again, this time by Roy's powerful command. He was not three yet. And not trained (I had started you at one. And Roy had resisted.)

I said to Roy, "You will join Neil in preschool when you go to the bathroom by yourself." Roy was trained that same day. Look at the power of love.

And when it came to Naseem, I was much more initiated into trauma!

Love,

Your ever-learning mom

In Search of a
Soul in a Human
Computer

I get lost abroad and at home, at will. I have found out that the underlying driving force for me to repeat this, is to re-experience myself and my interactions with the world when I was born.

This time, I want to be an observer while also participating. What was this undeciphered, colossal intricate software, with a hidden soul? How did I perceive being in the world and react to it, and allow some influences by nature to activate my birth apps? And maybe learning a bit, just a bit, to awaken me to the existence of my soul.

Raising my children and witnessing my grandchildren's magnanimous liquid development have quenched the thirst only to some extent as I cannot pursue their souls. I am only amazed by the awesome potential with which nature has gifted them.

No different from Pinocchio, I am actively searching for my soul. And contrary to Peter Pan and his shadow, my soul cannot be sewn to my body. I also have no illusion of a wizard in the land of Oz.

Only by elusive episodes of chance encounters does it become crystal clear that it not only exists but that my soul and I are inseparable. Just enough to remind me that I have it. And, indeed, that it's always with me, if I could only shed my false self, all the unnecessary layers of protection and efforts to conceal my nature.

Getting lost and trying to find my way by asking directions from strangers is pitiful compensation for all the times I ignored or missed good suggestions and benevolent hints or advice. My second name could be "Regret." But I don't have time for that. There is no time or energy in my system to nurture regret. Just move on with liquid time, which inevitably sees me commit a new regrettable act amongst all the enlightening new experiences. Regrets are tangible proof of our humanity and its limitations in the face of unlimited potential. So, let's just move on and get lost.

I ask a stranger for directions as if I am practicing paying attention. But still I don't follow them. Then I ask another one. It's because I am lost in me, not in the outside world. I am disoriented in my inner labyrinth. The only way I can get in touch with my soul is to exit my labyrinth. And yet there is no Minotaur to be slayed. My Minotaur, my maze, and my Theseus are the same. Like the conversion of particles, light, and waves in nuclear physics. It depends what you are consciously searching for - then you'll see that version.

Another collateral pleasure of travelling is seeing different versions of myself reflected in different circumstances. When lost in various corners of the planet, I feel exhilarated to communicate with my counterparts, some of whom look totally different from me, most of the time without a common spoken language. It's like the less I know the more authentic my experience will be. The beautiful toothless young woman in Transylvania who took me to my right destination, the Lavash swirler in Armenia who lovingly gave me a freshly baked loaf of bread, the Arab bus owner in Jordan who brought me mango juice when I refused coffee, the Berber in Morocco who implied I was worse than a Berber when I tried to bargain him down for a little piece of fragrant sandalwood. In each instance, we lacked a common language. But their piercing gazes connected us.

All were versions of me under different circumstances. Less language gives more potency to communication, my fascination with words notwithstanding.

I have been more than few times placed, by powers beyond me, near a person who had uncanny similarities to me. A total stranger and yet familiar. All versions are so lovable or forgivable, or pitiable. None are to be abhorred, even though some must be avoided.

Like the young British swindler who darted toward my train compartment after spotting me in a railway station in Bucharest, introducing himself as a lawyer who was now a fugitive, sitting on millions of pounds after protecting a criminal client. His expensive and stylish clothes were so unlike those of a tourist like me. I have a simple MRI and X-ray apparatus, just simple words, that identifies the educational background of people, not their innermost treasure of virtues and swamp of vices. His was limited to elementary education. His MRI had given him a clear scan of my naiveté. The intriguing story he had woven, which could be unraveled with slightest inquiry, was used with a purpose in mind. I never learned of his purpose.

Maybe, as he mentioned the nice girl he had met in Serbia who had given him free accommodation and storage, he was enticing me to do the same. He had identified similar gullibility in both of us, something he laser focussed on as a means to his survival. He was not abhorrent to me, just to be avoided. We parted in Brasov just before I took the bus to Bran village to see the medieval fortress built at the edge of a cliff. In popular belief, it's the designated location for the fictional Dracula, a novel by Bram Stoker.

It was only later that it dawned on me that not only I was sitting beside a real Dracula on the train, but was entertained by him, as well. A modern Dracula. Was it a force of nature to confront me with the fact that he could be one of my versions? The other side of the coin that carries my naiveté.

Is it the way I perceived the world and interacted with it during my early, formative years? So naive, so unsuspecting, so curious, so hopeful and trusting toward my fellow humans. All of my versions. Like I had embraced life despite feeling lost in it, searching for my soul.

Maybe even as beautiful as the little girl in South Africa, with a velvety ebony face studded with two glittering diamonds of eyes, sending me sparkles, who told me, "Give me something. Give me anything."

The other day, early in the morning I was standing at the corner of my driveway securing the lid of the compost bin for collection later in the day. I noticed how sunny this day in late December was, under a pale blue, cloudless sky. The sparrows were chirping jubilantly, as if busy preparing the nest to be egg-friendly for spring, and some young green was forcing itself out of the nurturing frozen soil beneath the powdery snow. It was as if, right at that moment, the seasons were mingling together. I drank the fresh crisp air. Time was so liquid. Past, present, and future fused. I felt my soul. It's always with me. I don't need to get lost anymore—but, like an addict, I may get lost for the sheer exhilaration of it.

Google my colossal computer of brain with its massive archive: What is soul? Click on search. It jams up.

Ah! They say we can only use 10 percent of it.

GLORIOUS CARTHAGE
AND ITS DAYLIGHT
BANDITS

Tunisia went to the top of my list of places to visit after I learned about General Hannibal's business and strategic acumen. The ancient Tunisia, Carthage, was a business hub during his active years and long before him. He won wars, but his strategies and business interests were not soaked in blood.

One of the best army commanders of the ancient world, Hannibal was interested in expanding trade with Mediterranean people, carrying his cargo of tin ore, a necessary element for producing bronze, and far more, over 2,000 years ago by land and sea. That's how my romance with General Hannibal started.

I arrived in Tunis on February 7, 2016. My hotel was a bank from the French era that had been converted into an old-style boutique space in the old city centre. Medina's main street connected the abiding old civilization to the French-dominated part. I checked in and went for a walk.

It was early afternoon and the main street and its shops had obviously seen better days. To my right was the timeless city with narrow walkways and mud structures comprising a bazaar. There was no hustle or bustle here. I considered an oval blue ceramic serving dish a young merchant offered for half price, noticing my lack of enthusiasm. Later in a little eating place, the proprietor pointed to the only free seat, and I shared a table with a polite young man while other men were watching, making me aware that despite there being no restriction in dress code, custom required more prudence from me. The slow-cooked lamb in spices was delicious.

I walked a bit more along scorched semi-residential mud roads separating small, humble walled houses with a few variety stores scattered in between, and returned to the hotel before sunset.

I studied the map of the city and area. The remains of Carthage are located in an elevated patch of land accessible by a local train, ten minutes' walk from the hotel.

I dreamt to see Matmata where Troglodyte, underground Berbers, lived. And Malta, and much more in the last three days before departure.

At 6 a.m., I had a nice buffet breakfast in the old bank lobby with a high dome-shaped ceiling made of beautifully patterned stained glass.

A pleasant woman sitting nearby with her husband, for some reason, took an interest in me and came to my table; she announced that they were in Tunisia to sell their last property and leave. They were Italian and had wintered there for decades and run businesses but they believed the country was becoming unstable. I felt she was trying to alert me, perceiving me to be vulnerable.

I went back to my room to brush my teeth, and said au revoir to the desk person who was fluent in English. The birds were singing and the air was fragrant from the trees, but I did not know which kind. As I exited the hotel in a light dress and felt the beautiful, crisp morning without the sun to be a bit chilly. I went back inside and put on my windbreaker. It was now about seven o'clock. I checked my handbag and put the tiny holder that held my Visa card and room key card in my windbreaker pocket for easy access when I reached the ticket kiosk. The stores were closed and there were just a few people walking and fewer cars on the road. I was pleasantly hit by the fragrance of Narcissus in huge bundles from the field to be distributed in the city.

The train station was a few steps ahead. The train was filled to capacity. All were locals throwing side glances. Tunisians are Semites, a dark shade of Caucasian with delicate features. They speak Arabic and French fluently. I had rarely felt in all my travelling such a compelling sense that talking was not advised. Most women were modestly dressed but none with a hijab. The train was in its last days, but it was clean like the streets in the city. It stopped at a transfer.

There was almost an hour's wait before the next train for Carthage arrived. It was as wrecked and slow.

It was 10 a.m. when it arrived on the street leading to the road to Dome Museum, the seat of Hannibal.

I asked a man for directions, and with polite disinterest he said, "Au bout!" At the end of the street.

I missed the easy intersection and got lost for about an hour walking along what seemed to be a major street, active with light traffic and a few pedestrians. It started to rain and I was happy to be wearing my windbreaker. A golden sun was shyly moving to take centre stage in the cloudless, light blue sky.

By the time I found my way to the short road that engulfs the museum, I noticed some Arabic chatter behind me. My instincts registered some concern. The volume of the voice indicated that the people behind me were keeping a steady distance. I looked back and saw two local men in their late twenties, with athletic builds, one taller, both well dressed. Our eyes met and I said hello. They responded.

I continued and noticed they were coming to the same street, which leads to the Dome, a tourist site, rather than following the path to the train station. Then they sped up and started walking a few steps ahead of me. The second bell rang.

As we approached the entrance of the museum, across the street, one turned back and said in good English, "Do you want me to take a photo of you?" My instincts rang the third bell. I was walking along the side of the road, which merged with a densely treed, forest-like area sloping toward the main road along which I just had walked. I

85

moved toward the middle preparing to cross the street, watching for slow and occasional cars and said, "No, thank you. I have arrived." He said "No! It's farther!" I paused in confusion for a second and then kept walking.

It was a matter of a split second before he turned back again, looked into my eyes, and suddenly pounced. He covered my mouth with one hand; with the other, he kept my shoulders immobile, while pulling me toward the treed area. The other one had walked one more step and was now in front of me, pulling my handbag, which I was holding onto reflexively for dear life.

I don't know it was me who let the handbag go or the pressure on my shoulders that loosened my grip, but it was a lifesaving moment as they both ran like wild animals. I fell down at the edge of the road like a rag doll, though not because of any harsh blow to my body. Indeed, they had handled me with minimum body contact as the penalty for theft would be much less compared to any unwanted touch of a woman. Islamic law. The whole ordeal, which felt like eternal damnation and humiliation lasted fewer than thirty seconds.

I got up feeling emotionally dizzy and took a step to the road, screaming for help. A local lady driver who noticed me stopped, made an expression of immense sorrow, and helped me into her car. She drove to a nearby tourist police station, which I had noticed earlier. They were most sympathetic and sorrowful as they had surrounded the museum for the safety of tourists but had missed this one.

The daylight robbery of tourists had become a trade. The police were doing their best to match the information with photos of the offenders, but there were too many of them, mostly young men, and a few women. The police believed they only wanted money, and not passports or any objects, even iPhones.

But all was gone now, except my little pouch with my Visa card and hotel key.

The police drove me to the Canadian consulate and, noticing my agony, insisted on driving me back to my hotel in the old city, collecting my belongings, and transferring me to the airport without a new passport. But they needed the Canadian authorities to allow this. The support was not granted, and I had to wait three more days in an absolute emotional concussion until my new passport was issued.

Once it was done, I managed to go back to the old bazaar and buy that blue ceramic dish and some locally roasted coffee before going to the airport.

Six months later, I was visiting Iceland.

Do I dream that one day I may go to Carthage, Matmata?

AGELESS STORIES: GOD, ARE YOU TALKING TO ME?

It was a privileged era, my childhood. Filled with stories. Of parents, aunts, uncles, and nannies, and sometimes made by ourselves. Nothing original. All timeless. All borrowed precious gems worth cherishing and never thinking of claiming them as our own. They belonged to nature and could as easily inhabit our minds as they had in nature. Now that I think of it, nature belongs to them. We belong to them.

Among many fascinating tales, the one that was planted in my mind and kept growing, making an impression throughout my life, was by my brother Farhat. It proved to be ageless, having the nature of developing as my neurons did. My neurons have started going through decay, but the story keeps harvesting more fragrant flowers and juicy fruits.

Only a year and a bit older than me, Farhat was endowed with a learning capacity worth being a progeny of dirt.

I don't know at this time whether any word of the story in my mind was told to me by little prepubescent Farhat, but for sure he told me the story. The essence of it was recounted to me in fewer than thirty seconds, after he had read it somewhere—most probably a Persian translation of Quran verses. Farhat was always in a rush. As if he was actually running with real time and not wanting to waste any of it. Indeed, he had little time for me. Although he saw the potential in me, he had little patience for my head being turned against facts. He would dart in and dart out. Deliver the goods and trust that sometimes it could be understood by me. His whole life, for me, felt like this.

Here it is, what has been built on his story. Just one addendum. At the dawn of struggle in English language to come with a third person gender, neutral pronoun, I'll borrow the ready-made Persian "Oo." (او)

God, the master sculptor, was enjoying life by perpetual creation. They were all knowing angels who bowed to Oo upon coming to life. The result was progressively getting better as Oo dared to try more fragile materials. But time came when Oo had exhausted all matters from soap stone to precious metals to precious stones. Forlorn and bursting for creative work, suddenly it downed on God that Light, a pure Energy form can be tried.

The result was so magnificent that Oo called all the angels to come and see the new creation, the one dearest to Oo because of lacking any matter, just light. It was a very challenging endeavour. God called the new creation Lucifer, meaning "light bringing." What an apt name. It was made from the light and like Morning star, planet Venus, it twinkled from the depth of darkness. Like all other angles, Lucifer bowed to God and appreciated being the dearest to Oo's heart. So, for a while heaven was in a joy ride. All angles happy with their ranks, and God's unconditional love, even though Lucifer had centrality in celestial order. Damn centrality!

Soon the pain of boredom caused by the sameness in heaven, made Oo yearn for another creation. But nothing was left. In near despair God noticed the lowly earth, totally unfit for artistic creation. But there was no other option.

Oo went to work. Something may come of it. It's so base that it should have some unforeseen valuable quality, Oo thought in never-vanishing optimism. Master sculptor called the new creation Adam and realized that it was undoubtedly dumb. All the myriad angels, including Oo's dearest one, Lucifer, knew Oo innately. This one did not seem to recognize its creator. No, it was not omniscient like the others. Therefore, it had to be protected by the capacity to learn. God thought life would be in perpetual amazement with this last one. Not a boring moment anymore.

Oh, the mistakes it is going to stumble on before it learns about Oo the Almighty!

God called all the angels and explained the situation and about the difference between Adam and the rest of them. God wanted all to bow to this earthen object, emphasizing the distinct feature It had: capacity to learn which will take it to a unique journey to recognize the creator.

Adam had a soul walking in parallel, guiding it to the right path. All the other angels did not need to have such a soul.

All the angels bowed with reverence and humility. All took a protective position toward this crippled creature in need of a soul. But Lucifer was defiant. He did not bow. God tried to cajole but failed. Lucifer was getting angry and dejected meteorically. God! Are you talking to me? Your most beloved angel? You want me with substance of light, to bow to dirt?

This genre of feeling, rage, did not exist in heaven. There, it was all about appreciation, gratitude, and humility. The dearest angel was going to war to restore his original status. No matter of explanation helped. There was a serious misunderstanding. How could God's most precious creation, made from pure light, be so insecure in the presence of a worthless, ignorant piece of dirt? It took so much time to make Lucifer, but just a jiffy to make a human.

Lucifer wowed to use the same virtue that makes the piece of dirt superior to light—its learning capacity, its soul—to steer it away from its creator.

The rest is history. Lucifer became the prince of darkness, Mephistopheles, Satan, and a few more. And humans had to navigate right from the wrong in search of meeting their soul to elevate their base origin, and reach the Almighty.

No wonder Farhat did not waste time in pursuits of purity. How could this young boy be aware from so early on that pursuits of purity only bring wrath and arrogance? It took me a few more decades to grasp that. It was in a search for purity that I stumbled on huge volumes of literature. My mistakes guided me to live my life and get a soul.

The piece of dirt moving toward light to see its dirt more. Lucifer, the light giver, the essence of purity, vying for the piece of dirt's soul. They are so much in tandem. Is there really such a dichotomy? A devil and angel?

Did our ancestors make up these stories to help us find our souls? To move from self-absorption to self enhancement?

It was my good luck to be raised with Farhat in the same era. His soul was filtered by light.

ANGELS COME IN
VARIOUS SHAPES
AND FORMS

I had a disabling spastic cough, though I was otherwise in a great state of health, for three days, and stubbornly wanted it to leave my system at my command!!

Yesterday the very young Chinese Uber driver became concerned about my cough. With limited language but massive communication power, he said, "You don't have a cold. What you have is asthma. It's allergies. I'll stop at a pharmacy."

Oh my God, I had been diagnosed finally. The culprit was an old hydrangea causing asthma-like spasms.

He told me, "You're old and you must exercise. Cardio and take oil." I expressed my utter appreciation for his generous sympathy and precious advice for sport and cod liver oil.

This early morning, I had the privilege of going for a walk with two young physicians to Edwards Gardens. Both mothers of very young children.

The garden's blossoming trees, whatever was left of trilliums, its massive number of tulips, Narcissus, and daffodils, a caressing sun, a deer coming toward us fearlessly, a falcon perching on a close-by branch, with the background music of Wilket Creek and cardinal and robin songs—all were dwarfed only by the enchanting company of my friends.

Both rapidly diagnosed an asthma-like spasm and suggested a puffer. They told me I most probably had a cold but that I must see my doctor. I would. If the absence of old hydrangeas did not bring recovery.

It was just after 9 p.m. of the same day when the doorbell rang.

An angel, a busy mother of two young daughters, a devoted physician, had brought me a puffer.

Shirin joon, you are precious and sweet.

The day after I saw my doctor and I had no symptoms. She diagnosed me as having recovered from a cold but somehow getting asthma-like spasms. But I am sure the hydrangeas and pollen in Edwards Garden had a role.

I had the same incessant spastic cough again walking in another pollen-rich park a few days later. The spring was unusually heavy with pollen. I had previously had no reaction to pollen. It was all over the streets. Thank God I had my puffer.

It was good the taxi driver had been right. "I am old!"

TAORMINA WAS
A MUST

All the Light We Cannot See is an intriguing story of a blind girl during World War Two in a small historic town in France's Brittany, called Saint-Malo.

Of all the painstaking work done by author Anthony Doerr regarding electromagnetic and radio waves ("all the light we cannot see"), what got my attention were the intricate cobblestone alleys and small shops the young blind girl keeps walking through that he describes. I had an unrelenting desire to see this sea-surrounded walled city. Just to walk on its little streets. And I did. And it was worth it.

It had far more ambiance than I expected as the end of summer had not stopped tourists and so business was vibrant. Families, mostly French, had infiltrated the narrow spaces between hotels, restaurants, shops, and residential areas, which were darkened by age and a bit green with algae. Ruins and modern construction mingled all over. From the elevated part one could see the clusters of beach lovers in very accessible seasides. A tame Mediterranean.

Here, during World War Two, this town in France was saved by its strategic position.

But I knew from the start that, even with some nearby castles, statues of war heroes, statesman such as Cartier, and writer and politician Chateaubriand, two days would be the longest I could spend there, given my patience.

Fortunately, my travel mate, my younger sister, was far more research oriented and thorough but equally motivated to see more. Why not seeing Paris and Sicily? My sister and I both love opera and knew Sicily had the oldest opera house.

We both agreed that Paris was decaying. Since our last trip there when I was robbed, Paris had become greyer. I still question why it's called the City of Lights. The marketing for tasteless, dry, long baguettes was as vigorous as ever. And after Saint- Malo, Paris felt like trap. Even walking along the Seine was not inviting for us to stay longer.

Sicily, in the same Mediterranean Sea but a world different, untame-able, made up for it all. A boat ride along its violent border, with a beach made of rough boulders forming cave-like spaces, reminded me of Odysseus. Being captured by one-eyed Cyclops, he used his legendary tricky nature to save his men from certain death.

Cyclops asked him, "What is your name?" Thinking of him as his dinner, Odysseus answered, "My name is Nobody."

A short while later, Cyclops' only eye was pierced by Odysseus. He cried for help from his brothers in nearby caves. When they asked him who blinded him, he answered, "Nobody!" They took it as a joke and did not come. While Odysseus instructed all his men to grab the belly of the sheep exiting the cave so Cyclops could not touch them.

But the whole of Sicily was filled with intrigue, enchanting with its natural beauty and ancient history, repeatedly ravaged by wars.

We were advised not to miss Taormina and we did go there. It was unbeatable. A little ancient volcanic village with smoke actively coming out of a visible volcano, Mount Etna. A very fertile hilly land.

It's elevated and reached by serpentine roads from the train station. Bus service for tourists is as busy and available as the restaurants and hotels. A real tiny place. Riddled by boutique sized stores for locals as well as tourists. One emblematic feature all over is the head of an African national usually wearing a turban. Sicily was overcome and captured by African rulers but eventually was saved by its own resistance and endurance.

The day we arrived at the Taormina walking towards our hotel, I noticed a sign on an ancient wall reading "Turandot: September 18," a few steps from our hotel. In my fatigued mind I thought: *Ah, so bad. Too late for us.*

It was September 17!

The day after, we took a tour to Palermo and more, after walking on the tiny central street and having a nice breakfast, which was included in our hotel fee. The majority of tourists were Italians.

The tour was far away and the day too hot. We saw an old opera house in Palermo. I also momentarily dipped into the quiet corner of the Mediterranean. I could not have missed it.

It was 7:30 p.m. when we returned to Taormina and we were walking toward our hotel along the little central street when suddenly my sister said, "Wow! Turandot is tonight at 8 p.m.!" It was like a bong to my head. Similar to the same bong that heralds the beheading of the hapless suitors who fail to answer the riddle designed by Turandot.

But I came to my senses. I said to my sister to rush to take a shower while I went to see if any tickets were available. We were both marinated in our own sweat.

Within a minute I was in the ticket area, a separate place from the opera house, which was still invisible to me. Two tickets in a middle row were available. They were snapped and I was on the run to deliver the good news, after hastily asking for directions to the opera house.

One minute of showering was enough for me. Right at 8 p.m., we arrived at the opera house. The evening was still bright. There was no sunshine, moonshine, or stars.

The opera house was an old amphitheatre with a capacity for 1,000 people. All seats were made of large stones and mortar. We sat on our stone seats, which were generously cushioned by a soft cover.

Above our head, minute by minute, darkness settled and a canopy of stars became our virtual ceiling.

The opera did not start at 8 p.m. They had to wait for dark so the bright and colourful stage became like a jewellery box.

Here, the Turkic-Mongol princess, as usual, was represented as Chinese with all Chinese stage paraphernalia. And the ear-deafening bongs.

The performance was superb.

It was a dream come true.

Melodic Sicilian voices, a Roman amphitheatre, a most beautiful starry sky, with close to a 100 percent Italian audience to capacity.

The next two days we enjoyed more day and night scenes, and more delicious authentic dishes. A few weddings in nearby churches were the icing on the cake of our happiness.

Relying on the Kindness of Strangers: Singing Vincero in Amman's Airport

The little makeshift landlocked country of Jordan is a melting pot of ethnicities—generally Semitic people from a Caucasian root. It's not a mosaic like Canada, encouraging diversity and differences. Like today's U.S., people have to adapt by blending rather than stay different.

Just a short period of mingling with random people is enough to reveal that the native Jordanian Bedouin are outnumbered by refugees from war-ravaged nearby Arab countries. There may be some differences in ethnicities, but they're not apparent to the uninitiated tourist. The dress code is conservative but relaxed with no iron-fist threat. They speak various dialects of the Arabic language.

The university students who wanted to celebrate New Year's Eve with me were from Jordan's neighbours. The cheerful sixteen-year-old who guided me to the right bus was from Palestine, for example, and the young medical school graduate working as a grocery store clerk who escorted me to the right taxi was from Syria. All spoke sufficient English to communicate with me flawlessly.

Taxis were dirt cheap, and on the roads were plenty of the old, beaten-up ones—but they were still clean. The cabs were always playing the most soothing Bedouin songs, and the drivers were generally nearly illiterate. My hotel was a bit out of town, although I walked only fifteen minutes to bring myself to the centre of Amman, the capital city, once I learned the intricate multileveled road. But calling a taxi by hotel concierge cost as much as an airport limousine in Toronto. Of course, those taxis were in better shape.

I had a greedy and busy sightseeing schedule, which I made ad hoc every morning. With half an hour here and there wasted and some mistakes, I accomplished a lot in a few days.

The night before my departure, I came back from Petra, a complete day trip. The taxi driver was a quiet man, a nondescript local with no knowledge of English. The drive was very pleasant, with lovely Bedouin songs playing on the radio. It was rather late in the evening. I don't know what got to me that I wanted this driver to take me to airport next evening.

All I had to tell him was, "Please be here at 8:30 p.m. tomorrow and take me to the airport." With all the ingrained Arabic words in the Farsi language, the gift of Arabs conquering Iran and ruling it for centuries, and with all my dismal secondary school Arabic knowledge, and having exercised it in multiple places, I could not remember how to say the number eight in Arabic, never mind 8:30. "Hotel" and "airport" were easy!

But in fewer than five minutes using mime and my fingers counting, the driver nodded that he understood me. And I trusted him, as it's my nature to prevent facts from getting in the way of my path.

The next day, I had another fact eliminated plan and yet all was accomplished. And thanks to young Syrian doctor finding me the right cab, I was at hotel at 8 p.m. I rushed to shower and get dressed, and fetched my carry-on.

At 8:20 p.m., I was outside the hotel, now more sober after the events of the day. And the "facts" of my situation started to loom in my mind. How on earth had I expected the taxi driver to be here? We had not communicated at all except by mime.

I thought if I asked the hotel concierge to call a cab for me, I would still be at the airport by 9 p.m. for my flight at midnight.

I threw a last glance, knowing it was not 8:30 p.m. yet and, lo and behold, saw the taxi standing right where I'd been dropped off the night before. The nondescript driver was looking at me in a familiar way, and with a faint smile, through the dark of the evening.

All the way to the airport, I was lulled by Bedouin songs, in otherwise absolute silence. We arrived at the airport where the taxi driver had to pay the toll to bring me to the entrance.

I remembered then that I had forgotten to convert my Jordanian dinars back to dollars, and I had plenty of them. Far more than the Toronto airport limousine fare. All was rightfully the property of my good Bedouin driver. We both said "Shokran!" A simple "thank you" was exchanged.

As I stepped toward the airport entrance, the Bedouin music in my ears was replaced by a leitmotif of "Vincero, Vincero, Vinccro!" from the opera *Turandot* in my brain. Don't they say it's not over until the fat lady sings? Well, here, after the elimination of so many facts, I had arrived at the airport on time—however improbably! The fat lady, in the case of this opera, the fat man, raised his song.

I was so happy that my musical cells had activated one of the most beautiful operas by Puccini, based on a masterpiece of storytelling by twelfth-century epic romantic Persian poet Nezami, and adapted by the German poet Schiller. Turandokht, mutilated by translation and pronunciation, turned into *Turandot,* and it still fills the heart with what Nezami conveyed in his masterpiece "Seven Beauties" (Haft Paykar.) One story for each day in the week and named after a planet.

Nezami is truly holistic and conciliatory. He weaves past and present, ethnics and cultures, tragedies and fulfillment. In the Monday story, in Red (Mercury), an incognito Persian prince, Bahram (changed to Kalaf in the opera), during his exile, seeks the hand of a Turkish-Mongol (in the opera, Chinese) princess for his bride—not for love, but for influence peddling to save his uncle from jail. He has to participate in a deadly competition that has already slaughtered many hopeful young men. Turandokht had devised three riddles that, if not answered correctly, would cause the suitor to be executed. What a humiliation for Turandokht when the winner is declaring his victory, but no love.

But my Vincero had a lot of love for Jordan and Jordanians. I did not sleep during my long flight that night—not out of fear of the raging Turandokht but because of simple insomnia.

Stories from Rehab: No Safety at Home or Away from It!

I was sitting in the spartan lounge of rehab, reading.

My injured, braced left leg was held up in a horizontal position by versatile devices on my wheelchair. I wore a yellow tag, which meant I needed support and supervision.

The space was very limited but I could go around and face the balcony opening to the beautiful serene green of the rehab grounds and a willow tree with branches dancing to the gentle September wind.

I noticed a woman and a young man coming in and sitting around the table, facing me. She made easy eye contact.

So easy that, after I greeted her, she told me she and her son were waiting for her husband's room to be prepared. An untimely stop by a car had caused a crash, crushing her husband's legs.

She told me that she was a kindergarten teacher in her native Bangladesh and that the whole family was musical. She talked about it with such pride. She was so soft and transparent that I dared to ask her if she could sing me a song and if I could videotape her for my friends. She nodded her agreement as sweetly as the weeping willow branches in the wind. I videotaped her singing a nostalgic tune.

Later, I learned about a flood in Bangladesh and when we met in the hall again accidentally, I inquired about her husband and the flood.

She said she was aware of it and was very active in sending support. The song she had sung was not only a prayer regarding her husband's injury but a collective prayer for all.

Lyrics: Pray to God for all the beautiful flowers that celebrate life. She certainly is one.

CREOLE, GUMBO, HURRICANE, AND ALL THAT JAZZ

I am not sure when was the first time I heard about a Creole dish called gumbo, but I certainly did not know anything about Creole. But the first time I had gumbo was in Jack Astor's at Shops at Don Mills, Toronto, during the Quebec festival of Mardi Gras, the year of Hurricane Katrina (which took place in August 2005). I happened to go for a conference to New Orleans, the recipient of the deadliest attack of this tropical cyclone, the year after. The media still talking about the mismanagement of the hurricane's aftermath, death toll, catastrophic destruction, and the people who had become homeless.

Although the downtown had remained untouched and had suffered no structural damage, it felt like the spiritual gut of the city had been removed. The media's perpetual reports of devastation seemed hollow compared with the emotional experience one would go through in real time. On the surface, tourism was active and business looked normal. The conference hotel was opulent and brochures encouraging sightseeing were plenty.

In off times from the conference I had planned to do a few things: taste an authentic seafood gumbo, see the places destroyed by the hurricane, listen to jazz (although I had little interest in it—after all,

I was at its birthplace), and visit the blue bayous, associated with a romantic song, and their alligators.

Tours of ghost-infiltrated graveyards and the red-light district, highly advertised by the tourism authority, were of no interest to me, though the deep sadness in the city would make visiting cemeteries an appropriate activity. Without any intention, however, I visited both and was glad I did not pay for a tour.

The gumbo soup experience was utterly disappointing.

Creole, an ethnicity with Latin origins that means creation or the sudden birth of new from older elements, in New Orleans, embodied some aspects of the culture, people, and cuisine. The sudden birth of *new* in New Orleans was parented by the forced exile of the poor, unhinged French, who were put in prisons as convicts and prostitutes. They were used to populate the new French colony. France, under the reign of Louis XIV, who went bankrupt and was totally unable to exploit its vast colony, resorted to manipulating its people—first, by promising gold and silver, and when that failed, by capturing disenfranchised French and sending shiploads of them to Louisiana (the namesake of King Louis). This was in 1713, when Britain took over Acadia in Canada and exiled French Canadians went to Louisiana, as well. Acadia was transformed to "Cajun" or "Cajan." All of this happened eighty years before Louis XVI and Marie Antoinette were beheaded.

Creole was born from the forced togetherness of mostly French prisoners, Cajuns, Black people, and the natives who kindly fed and sheltered them. Creole is almost the opposite of diversity. It's blending, the opposite of today's cherished diversification.

Gumbo is a famous and delicious creole dish, a thick soup. It includes onion, garlic, lentils, okra, tomatoes, shrimp, and sometimes chicken. No gumbo in New Orleans followed the recipe. One consistent ingredient was potatoes! I am ever so grateful to Jack Astor's for giving me the most authentic gumbo.

The boat ride in the bayous of New Orleans along a slow stream of almost still water with some plantation, fish, and occasional alligators in a motionless state, was managed by a strong though out-of-shape local man whose breath reeked of alcohol. He told us how the whole land was a vast swamp that slowly got drained. He also said that oak, a major resource, had become scarce. The bayou had a blue reflection to its surface—thus, the inspiration for the famous song.

The long tour along the hurricane-destroyed area was very close to the oceanfront. Indeed, someone's first thought might be: *Who would ever choose to live here in the first place?* Who but people who come to the "Big Easy," for low-paying jobs in tourism and hospitality, who see the deserted, ruined shack-like structures as a free roof. Who but people who knew little of the predictable, perennial hurricanes? It felt like they were returning ghosts of hungry French people who had been exiled there in 1713.

I noticed the smart draining system in our hotel and other old, established places, which would never allow any accumulation of water and its forceful attack if it ever reached them. Was a hurricane the culprit or poverty?

I was searching for a restaurant or bar with jazz music, walking along a major street when I heard lively music some distance ahead. The farther I went, the louder the jazz until it came to its loudest and then started to go soft. I could not identify any bar or restaurant to enter and listen to this rapturous, soul-drenching music. Soon, the sound became too faint so I retraced my steps and it became louder and louder before it again went faint.

In my third retracing after failing to see any place where the music originated, I just stopped and did not move when the music became the loudest. I was under an oak tree bearing a spreading canopy of branches with dense foliage of dark green, elongated leaves, befitting of the midsummer season. The jazz musicians were inhabiting the tree. Little black birds, hundreds and hundreds of them, were invisible to me, but their music was the softest jazz I had ever heard. A silky, jazzy brass music that was comforting to the soul. I wondered if the earlier jazz musicians had gotten their inspiration under similar trees. I stayed under the oak tree enjoying free-for-all jazz, no longer in search of a jazz bar. Fearing disappointment, I have not ventured into any jazz venue since.

STORIES FROM REHAB: STOCKHOLM SYNDROME REVISED

Terribly frightened by regression fostered by a caregiving environment, I have tried to maintain a modicum of independence. Still under the influence of narcotic painkillers, I claimed my ability to wash my hair and back. I dusted the little table beside my bed. I vigorously campaigned for my discharge and, with each rejection, felt like the criminal character in *Shawshank Redemption*. After thirty years in jail and meeting a white-collar criminal with a plan to escape, he was able to dupe the board of parole by no longer saying he was a changed person. He said, "Ladies and gentlemen, rehabilitation is BS. I'll never change."

But I did not know what my script should be. I could not feign disability.

I vacillated between the two innocent criminal characters in *Papillon*. I was neither Steve McQueen who never stopped escaping, nor completely resigned Dustin Hoffman.

And then suddenly the engine for my discharge started. I felt a pang of some discomfort in my gut. I did not want to leave!!!

Wow! I was right in the heart of the Stockholm Syndrome.

There was, however, absolutely no brainwashing in my captivity. Not the slightest sense of affection for anybody in rehab. So why didn't I want to leave?

It dawned on me that, after trauma, when our perceived sense of security and stability is shattered to zero, we are prone to grab anything that gives us a semblance of our memory of what security could feel like. Any repetitive occurrence had created a sense of familiarity, had made me feel life will be continued.

Yes, I am attached to the familiar sounds and visions in rehab. I can differentiate between the wheeling trolley of food and that of housekeeping. I can identify a hopper from a walker. I enjoy hearing the loving whisper of my neighbour from Sri Lanka with her husband. I am attached to announcements imploring visitors to leave as it's past 8:30 p.m. I enjoy young Ken bringing a cup of coffee for me exactly the way I like it, and a *Toronto Star*, each time he visits his wife next door.

I get ignited by mingling with teen volunteers. I am haunted by weeping willows' branches dancing to the breeze, when sitting in the lounge.

And how about twenty-year-old Savanah wheeling herself to my room, saying, "Knock, knock! Who is there? Let's knit together."

I feel ecstatic hopping or wheeling down the hall, seeing everyday people getting better and feeling excited to be discharged. It makes seeing the daily arrivals of casualties much easier. There is a lot of hope in this place.

I am attached to hope. But I know I'll carry it home with me.

Happy Women's Day

How far we have come with #metoo, but what about the boys?

In the wake of #metoo and all along its prime time in the U.S. and, later, in a more moderate way in Canada, I was sent into a reverie with a nightmarish hue.

Wow! How far we have come!

In Georgian England, the molestation and rape of women was a common practice, whether by rogues on a London bridge or employers of massive numbers of women who had the good luck to get work as domestic helpers.

Fast forward to my birthplace—Iran, twentieth century, and first-hand information.

It was like rite of passage. As soon as the first physical sign of feminine development appeared, innocent girls were targets of unwanted humiliating attention by socially deprived and depraved men. It was continued till old age as long as a woman was perceived beautiful or unprotected. These men made up a very small minority of an otherwise highly dignified male population, but the hurt they inflicted was enormous. It was like one virus causing an epidemic.

It would be comprised of terrifying ogling when one would feel being undressed in public by a swiftly walking man who brushed by too closely, along with actually being touched.

While parents were highly alert about protecting their daughters and would get into verbal fights and at times actual assaults with the offenders, it was an accepted social feature. It was like: "if you really don't want it, don't go out."

The busy streets of downtown Tehran and its buses were merciless with skilled predators. There was no protection even if a young woman was walking with two parents. The touching of their body, mostly around the hips, whether by the hand, hip, or genital area of an offender, was inevitable. It was predictable and unpreventable.

When I blossomed into a diminutive feminine form from my skinny childhood, I was mostly accompanied by a servant. A young man in uniform, my father being in the army, would walk behind me. That guaranteed me 100 percent safety. But not even when I was walking beside my parents was it safe. As a naive teenager, I would scream when I was touched but the culprit would be too difficult to identify. The skilled offender had a flat, "in his own world" facial expression that would make one doubt the accuracy of one's perception.

On many occasions, if a woman was accompanied by a man, the suggestion of molestation caused a street brawl or wrestling in the bus and the offender would brutally assault the defender. This forced women to keep the violation to themselves, not wanting their father, brother, friend, or husband be beaten to a pulp. Also, there would be an inaudible whisper in the air: "What did you do to provoke (stimulate) the thug?"

There was no social safety net. Everybody knew it existed, but it was too difficult to catch the offender, and there were too many of them. Again, I repeat the percentage of offenders was very small compared with dignified men.

Many young women, however, were aggressive enough to slap the predator and scare him away, but this act could have been reversed. It could be the woman who was assaulted further. Many like myself learned to pretend nothing had happened and just speed off.

There was at the very onset of molestation season, for a budding femininity, a brief moment when the pain of humiliation and violation was mingled with pride! Not joy or happiness. It felt like a man, a very lowly man, a very deprived man, was giving the licence of official womanhood in such a humiliating way. Then anger and helplessness, and later, nausea, and finally, numbness would set in. Like getting used to mosquitoes. That was perhaps closest to what a victim of incest feels.

Perhaps the endemic aspect of it did not allow it to be traumatic. Increasing age and experience reduced the incidence as our alertness prevented a bit of blind sighting aspect of the action. We could identify the offender only if he was facing us and then smoothly dodge his intent to touch "accidentally!" And remove ourselves fast if the offender was in the back, versus questioning what was happening and, in self-doubt, be molested more like when our physical femininity was dawning before our awareness of it.

Despite the lack of social sanction, individual girls and boys, like their European and American counterparts, went through the same stages of getting acquainted with the opposite sex, sometimes secretly and sometimes veiled by friendship—and rarely openly. The perverted male characters were a minority nestled inside the healthy mainstream.

And what about the boys? Their sexual abuse was much more severe. And I am sure that's how a young boy trapped by a degenerate man felt.

Those who were molested by pedophiles were usually killed, as the penalty for the offender would be an unceremonious death sentence. No witness could be left behind.

We watched movies and TV shows with rapt attention on how some Western women demeaned themselves by making themselves sexual props on the stage representing a socially normative feature. To us, it seemed a deliberate choice by the woman who wanted a job or whatever. It looked like that was endemic in the West. Demeaning women while the loud cry was for their liberation and independence. It was a contradiction in terms.

Mind you, this happened in Iran, too, but its incidence compared with molestation in the streets and buses was negligible. And, socially, it was absolutely frowned upon.

We had no idea what was happening to Christian boys at the hands of pedophile priests in holy churches in the West, nor of the systemic abuse of First Nation children in residential schools in Canada.

How far have we come?

In my last visit to Iran, in the early twenty-first century, as a woman past her physical prime, I was free from the mosquitoes!! Ah, old age brings so much advantage! But mosquitoes were all over, with the threat of serious penalty if ever they were caught. And they were reported by brave young women. No longer was the action of the thug supposed to be absorbed by the woman and converted to shame and anger.

But what about the boys? Abuse of boys had reached systemic proportions in the hands of pedophiles who were wearing religious garb and so were immune from punishment. As if some had gone to the Vatican for training.

With #metoo, one becomes hopeful that the dawn of women truly respecting themselves has arrived for the minority of Western sisters who were victimized by the societal norms of the time.

That is indulging in self-compromising actions when faced with predators who were and are made of the same fabric as depraved thugs in the streets of Tehran. And elsewhere.

And hopefully one day our boys will be more protected too and, like their female counterparts, will make #me too.

And women have to learn that they cannot go on slapping men's posteriors and thinking it's cute.

Stories from Rehab: Will-o'-the-Wisp . . . Love

In a weekend pass from rehab, as an experiment to see whether in a crippled form I could cope with real life, I went home. The house had to be retrofitted for a person who could not walk.

I am generally a menace to my children, who justly see me as a whirlwind of energy who gets fixed on doing, with no planning ahead, just improvising.

So, with one unplanned hop, I may lose my balance, fall, and re-injure myself.

This hopping was a serious business. One cannot hop over a one-inch barrier without heroic practice.

I was doted on, pampered, watched over, tenderly hugged and kissed by my three adult children.

My daughter, my spring breeze, kept whirling around me, admonishing, warning, kissing my forehead, feeding me delicious food she'd made for me.

This role reversal transported me in time.

I was determined to have six children, but I had to resign at three, having lost grip of the most unbending reality in life: time.

My husband, a modern, reality-focused man, wanted no more than two. Responsibility was his number-one concern. While atheist Dr. David Suzuki was trumpeting against procreation to control world population, he procreated five children. Why do people believe self-serving zealots?

For me, love, this will-o'-the-wisp, was the surest way out of my selfish corner, into a more enhanced form of selfishness. This responsibility was nothing but a consuming engagement with life. Not a burden. Three was the least I could accept. My selfishness was boundless.

I knew if we had a son and a daughter, that would be it. The set would be complete.

I prayed to God to give us two sons first so I could bargain for the third one, a daughter. A daughter for ME, please!

Soon, I realized, my imagined bargain was not happening. Meanwhile, I failed my specialty exam three times—effortlessly! Magical thinking came to help. I would not be worth having a daughter without passing my exam!

I passed my exam in no time.

And God gave me Naseem in nine months.

ALAS, MY DNA PORTENDS A GRIM PERSPECTIVE FOR HIDDEN POTENTIALS

I was morally vanquished by information made available to me by my friend Google … Or was it my well-guarded pride being pulverized?

My arrogance—I mean innate arrogance, unrelated to any worldly or spiritual achievement—has provided a lifelong internal battleground for me. The more I squash it and find my place as a totally average mortal, from dirt to dirt, the more liberated I feel. Like a speck of dust meandering through the wonderful universe.

One area, however, has failed me. In the innermost, faraway corners of my mind there are emotionally tangled cul-de-sacs not accessible for any negotiation with facts or reality. I am blue blooded. Just by the virtue of my DNA. I don't have to pay for any genome test. Long before me, my arrogant ancestors had taken care of it. It went directly to Abraham, Mohammad, and then landowners and serf keepers, and, finally, highly educated officials, culminating in a nineteenth-century Viceroy, the advisor to a dynasty, the penultimate diplomat, the essence of spiritual wisdom, the guardian of education.

"You must know the warp and weft of your existence. Pure gold."

This is pounded and tattooed in the mind of every descendent of Mirza Abol-Ghasem GhaemMagham. Royalty is generally from rogue blood, organically incapable of installation of morality and ethics in their psyche. They would do anything for money and the power to keep it—a simple fact easily evidenced by historical account of great empires. Just throw a glance at colonizing kingdoms.

When fate threw me in the loop of romance and marriage with a most humble Canadian psychiatrist with no impressive parentage, my father, the essence of humility, who loved my future husband, said with his poetic, tearful eyes: "You realize that you have stained the blue blood of your children. It's going to take 500 years for cleansing!" Alas, he did not live to learn that my children's choice of life partners extended the allotted 500 years to eternity. His poetic licence allowed him to assume that my children would find a Mirza Abol-Ghasem GhaemMagham for sure to claim back their blue blood.

Wait a minute. If Mirza Abol-Ghasem GhaemMagham DNA is so cleansing of rogue blood, then my heavily loaded blood should sanitize my children's blood very easily. And then my children's blue blood would cleanse their children's blood. What a relief! I was no different from my ancestors, whose concubines and their children, never mind their spouses, were issued instant passports to the Blue Blood region of the human kingdom.

My father, who was gifted with poetry, did not write down any of his poems. My mom did it after he passed away. He composed poetry when emotional and on demand, effortlessly. The poems came from the fire inside and turned to vanishing white curled debris moving in the warm air of his breath, like the particles after a fire. He could recite them any time he wanted. But for him it was not worth being written down compared with the treasures of poetry he had memorized from esteemed poets. One in lower rungs of ladder of poetry was Mirza Abol-Ghasem GhaemMagham.

Who was Mirza Abol-Ghasem GhaemMagham? Really, it's not a name. It denotes a position. Simply "Viceroy." He was elected by the ruling king to use his wisdom guarding the dynasty in early nineteenth-century Iran. His verse and prose are classic items in Persian literature. His dedication to education was such that he put his wealth in trust for deserving students who didn't have means, for generations to come. It's active to this day. Spiritually, he was so advanced that he had reached transparency of glass. He could see future. He predicted being murdered.

He was murdered by instruction of the same king he had guided and kept in power. Wow! Even now I feel humbled to be related to him. Or arrogant?

It was a pure accident when I googled Mirza Abol-Ghasem GhaemMagham and learned that through his well-thought plans and strategies he ordered the king's brother to be jailed and blinded to remove any chance of instability he was causing by claiming the throne. He also ordered a throng of young men to be blinded in order to squash any future retaliation. Let this be a lesson for future political dissents.

When I recently started to inquire about this "nonsense, false news" from my erudite siblings, they told me the information was accurate! How come I never learned about these brutalities? The answer was "What brutalities? He was bringing peace and order. He did it in the most humane way considering the norms in politics." Those young dissidents were openly executed a hundred years later during Shah's regime. And today, more secretly, in Iran.

Yes. Considering today's attack on Syria to protect its citizens from chemical gas used against them by their ruler, it seems that Mirza Abol-Ghasem GhaemMagham's action was relatively mild. And considering the loss of thousands of young lives, in civilians and army soldiers, in Afghanistan, to overcome murderous Taliban, and other atrocities in the name of bringing harmony and peace in human societies, his crime was minor.

And how we could ever forget two previous toxic gas attacks, and the use of smallpox-infested sheets that killed tens of thousands of innocent people?

And yet my blue blood is burdened by grim features down to receding history.

Did not Abraham, the fountainhead of my blue blood, try to kill his own son, born to a lowly concubine? He said it was for divine reason. That lowly son was rescued by divine power to continue the stream of blue blood in my ancestors. Did Mohammad marry a few concubines once his first wife died? She bore only one daughter, who carried the blue blood alongside a few lesser stepsiblings. And those on the opposite side of Islam see it heavily loaded with brutality.

Brutality and self-aggrandizement seem to be as essential features in rogue blood as in blue blood, only latter does it in style. May my children's blood be less blue. And may I be free from my pride by realizing that, despite its blue hue, my blood is quite ordinary. Amen.

STORIES FROM REHAB: ALL THINGS EPHEMERAL

When I opened my eyes and found myself lying flat on the street, I just sat up. Then I tried to stand up and noticed my left leg was not following my commands.

I heard somebody gently commanding me, "Don't move!"

I looked up and saw a First Nations woman looking down at me with concern (was she an angel?). Then I noticed there were also other people staring down at me.

I looked at my leg and saw that, under completely intact skin, it was detached from my knee. No pain! I was in shock.

I looked up and said, "Please call an ambulance." The First Nations lady (angel) said, "They have already called police and ambulance. Don't move!"

I could not. I willed my left foot again.

Within a few minutes, ambulance drivers were asking me to move.

"Put your foot down and walk. Nothing has happened!"

I loved what I heard. Nothing has happened. The car had just hit me while I was crossing the road on a solid green. But nothing had happened. My left leg, however, was not following me. I told the two young men, "I think a bone is broken and a tendon cut. I can't move my leg. I am going into shock." My teeth were chattering and my body was tremulous.

Seeing no blood and hearing no cry of pain, they remained sure that nothing had happened "You'll go home soon. You are just frightened and cold." It was early August.

In triage, a highly ornamented small man, perhaps a qualified nurse, who walked like a peacock, touched my left knee briefly and said, "Honey, nothing has happened. You'll go home tonight!" I was delighted to hear it! And yet I prayed to God that a doctor would examine me. My shakes were becoming violent, as if every cell in my body was summoned to preserve life. My teeth could have been chipped by involuntary rapid motion of my jaws.

Luckily, the doctor came soon and examined my left leg and said, "You are OK. We'll send you home tonight after the X-ray."

The ecstasy of me not being injured was competing with the violence of my shaking body that was fighting with my wishful thinking. Within a few minutes of the X-ray, the frightened face of the doctor ended my hope. My intactness became ephemeral. I would not be going home. And an injection of morphine stopped my shaking.

Hopping or wheeling myself around rehab, I am more accepting of my losses. One stands out with the severity of scorching sunshine. My three-times-weekly walk to pick up my grandchildren from daycare is no longer possible.

Gloating in my mind that I made five kilometres in forty-five minutes, I would arrive at the daycare, in summer or winter, my face salty and drenched in perspiration.

As I entered the toddlers' room, I would see a dozen of the freshest life forms just learning to walk. I would feel a cosmic love for them. I would want to hug them all. And they would flock to me! I would open my arms wide, as if I were to hug them all and suddenly I would see one of them—the sweetest life form, who was actually my not yet two-year-old grandson—flapping his arms, wobbling to me, and saying, "Grandma! Grandma!" Pulling my hand, and saying, "*You* are *my* grandma!" And I would dissolve!

It's not only the exhilarating walk that is lost. All of life's precious and treacherous moments are ephemeral. My grandchildren are growing and changing into different life forms with the speed of light, but still too fresh and scented heavenly. I better catch the passing moments.

Stories from Rehab: Beyond Prejudice

Among all the features of privilege in rehab is the service at its chapel, an eighty-year-old oak and stained-glass structure run by Anglican sisters. It's small and inviting. The volunteers and sisters make daily rounds, very softly inviting the injured fellows to join the service, usually mentioning songs and hymns related to healing, never failing to say it's for all faiths.

I like going to churches no matter where as I love to light candles. Here, there was no candle.

The chaplain was a tall slender woman in her sixties, with a stylish haircut, and on this Sunday, she was wearing a youthful long skirt and a top with sleeves up to her elbows.

She was eloquent, knew her sermons, and sang nicely to the piano music, and we accompanied her from the scripts we'd been handed.

We went through "Amazing Grace," "All Things Bright and Beautiful," "Were You There," and, finally, "The Lord of the Dance," a hymn I had not heard before. The short lyrics depict jubilation through dance. At this time, the chaplain started to wave her arms gracefully to the music and hold her skirt, making a semi-foxtrot turn and step.

While I was interestedly watching her ease among the rest of us in wheelchairs, I noticed both her forearms had large tattoos—one a life-sized green bird on a green stand, another a green palm tree in a tropical green landscape.

I had a flashback. A few minutes before I was wheeled to OR, my very personable young surgeon came to reassure me, and to introduce the anesthesiologist. As he turned around to go I noticed his athletic arms were covered with complex tattoos. I said a prayer for me!

If my daughter had brought his teen form to my house, I would have said loudly in my mind, "Please get out of my house!"

In his present form, a married father and skilled surgeon, he was someone I considered myself lucky to have as my physician. I saw the earlier angry teenager totally unaware of his God-given talent had finally found his call.

As for our lady chaplain, I see an earlier free-style hippie who also found her way and peace. I tried to overcome my internal bigot and told her it was courageous of her to display her tattoos. She kindly ruffled my hair(!) and with a sharp look made me hear loud and clear: "Baby, which planet are you inhabiting?"

I know my planet of liquid conflicts edging constantly toward prejudice. I try so hard to maintain my balance, though I get tripped perpetually.

STORIES FROM REHAB: ANGER IS A LUXURY I CANNOT AFFORD

Looking intensely at me and my injured leg, Dr. Mariam Vania, a friend and blessing in my life, wants to know exactly what happened in that fateful moment when I was hit by a car. After listening, she tells me, "If I were in such an accident, I would be very angry at the careless driver. I don't see any anger in you!"

She is a brilliant psychiatrist. She has made an accurate observation.

"Mariam, I want to use all my emotional resources to recover. I can't afford to feel angry," I tell her.

I travel back in time. February 2016. I was gagged and robbed by two young locals in Tunisia, in daylight in front of Castle, the ancient place where legendary Hannibal ruled the seas.

I cried.

Toward the thieves, however, I had no anger. They were professional thieves and being Moslems, they were most careful not to touch me except for the minimum required to get my handbag silently. Indeed, I was grateful for not having been violated in any other way.

I was angry at the Canadian consulate for being so indifferent to my demise.

Back in time, my son Roy, at age twenty-two, received a hefty scholarship to do a master's and PhD at Johns Hopkins. Within a few weeks, he was robbed at gunpoint in his very secure campus residence. I was so grateful to the thieves because they did not touch him. He was robbed of all his possessions, including his winter jacket. But the good thieves had left him intact.

I was angry at Johns Hopkins University for their total insensitivity, for not giving him the slightest support.

Yes, I *am* capable of experiencing anger. Over the years, however I have made a groove to divert the surge of anger toward the path of serenity as it's the most powerful factor in making the present worth living. And the present is all we have.

Taboos, Prejudices, and Lingering Hurt

Among social, cultural, religious, racial, and other taboos, the one that has left me with an enduring pain is the taboo of class.

Taboos are fossils of cumulative experiences that prove harmful over and over again, and thus, basically, are perceived as protective measures. They feel like red traffic lights and must not be ignored. We don't talk about them. We simply accept the forbidding and prohibiting aspects without questioning.

But time moves on and old taboos that ruled once get thrown away and replaced by new ones. Look at racism. At one time, interracial mingling was a taboo. Today, any hint of racism is a taboo. In 1946, Viola Desmond was a successful hairstylist and owner of a beauty school in Nova Scotia. She sat in the "White only" section of a movie theatre and was pulled out and fined for defrauding the government of a one-cent tax, rather than openly being accused of breaking the taboo of racial segregation. Today, Desmond's image graces the Canadian $10 note.

In 1955, little Claudette Colvin, only fifteen years old, and, later in the U.S., Rosa Parks, were challenged physically and in court for acting colour blind.

Taboos could be rooted in a family feud, like the tragedy of *Romeo and Juliet*. Or rooted in perceived social status differences like the

Persian love story of Shirin and Farhad. Countless broken-hearted young people have had to suffer in silence; many still do, if they fall in love with a person of a different religion.

Many brave people have stood for right action rather than succumb to a taboo that made no sense to them, but not me, when I was eighteen.

Our mother was a born educator. She never played a victim about having to study under the blanket with an oil lamp, taking enormous care not to be suffocated or cause a fire. All because in her neck of the woods, reading was a taboo for a woman. After four years of this heroic endeavour, she emerged with a high school diploma that made her instantly eligible to become the principal of a mixed elementary/secondary school.

The taboo had been dissolved by that time. She recalled that some of her fellow students were older and much taller and bigger than her. There and then, this little eighteen-year-old specimen of femininity shelved her signature loud laughter and converted her soprano voice to contralto, and her concerned stare to an ambiguous one, just to cover her fear. But it sure intimidated all her students. She ruled for four years.

Once she got married, she shelved her teaching career and dove into the most difficult profession: motherhood. That fulfilled her eternal thirst for learning.

Her natural inclination to educate, however, continued at multiple levels. Each summer when we vacationed in villages owned by her parents or my father's parents, within her budget, she carried antibiotics, fabrics, and one sewing machine.

God knows how many people were rescued from blindness caused by trachoma, endemic in that area. Many village women learned to sew professionally and started businesses for themselves. Each year, the sewing machine was gifted to the most talented and productive one.

At home, not only did she educate illiterate servants and maids, but all six of us had the duty to contribute to the process until they were able to get a certificate in elementary or secondary education.

Composition, math, reading, and correcting their papers were all assigned to us after she had established the foundation. Then she would help them get a job. On many occasions, she had found young people begging on the street and encouraged them to come for shelter, food, work, and study, each time reminding us that the "new employee" was not our personal servant. No personal orders, such as *fetch me a glass of water,* were allowed.

Once, we inherited a skilled cook from friends who were moving away. He was a small-built man in his late twenties with a deliberate policy of no eye contact. And he was an amazingly precious asset cherished by a family with three young girls. Looking at an unfamiliar woman was a taboo for a dignified man. His name was Lotfollah, meaning God's Grace, which was very befitting.

This was the first time we had a real cook, rather one trained by our mother. But his path was like that of the rest of illiterate workers. In the evening she started to teach him, and later in the course, we would merge. Lotfollah not only finished his diploma but took some college courses, and got a job in a pharmaceutical company.

Like the rest of our workers from whom we never heard after getting a job, nor ever expected to hear, Lotfollah disappeared into oblivion.

Two years had passed when Lotfollah rang in the late afternoon of a school day. My older brother and I had supervisory positions over the four younger ones, and six of us were sitting around the table doing our homework, with the TV off. My parents had not come home yet.

The most awkward and painful moments started. Lotfollah was neatly dressed, like a regular office worker. His eyes were still shut, except for short glances towards my brother, who was standing beside the hall door. My brother engaged him in conversation and eagerly asked him about his work, while pleading with his eyes with me: "What are we supposed to do?" It was as if we were begging each other to have the courage to ask Lotfollah to sit with us.

Taboo was rearing its ugly head. We had sat or stood beside Lotfollah to teach him but always in the kitchen or his own tiny place. Now the question of whether to ask a servant to sit beside us, even a former one was larger than life.

We had travelled a lot and developed a much humbler understanding of ourselves, and overcome the average prejudices at many levels. But this one, violating a status and class boundaries was beyond us. We were hoping that our parents would arrive soon, and release us from the torture of being such horrible hosts to such a nice human being. But Lotfollah left after telling us about his new life and hearing our delight, three of us standing awkwardly all the while.

When our parents heard about our dilemma, they admonished us: "Of course you should have invited him to sit and offered him tea!" And how much we suffered because we knew that's what we should have done, but for the reckoning red light of taboo? I kept hoping that if Lotfollah came again we would be far more human. The pain still lingers as he never came back.

Was the fossil of a taboo a self-protective measure on this occasion formed by the fact that my father's father was an incredibly modest, kind man who always mingled with his peasants, then was clobbered and paralyzed by them? He had insisted that the precious, scarce water in the village be distributed for irrigation to every serf. The bullies were offended.

It was the opposite case of Louis XVI and Mary Antoinette, who were decapitated when she suggested to hungry peasants that they should eat cake rather than whining for bread. If the economic diversity had not skyrocketed, maybe they would only have been clobbered, like my loving grandpa. Oh, my, the human mind can go too far to justify prejudice.

REMINISCING ABOUT MY DREAMY TEEN YEARS

I went to visit Atlanta and Savannah, Georgia, revisiting myself at age sixteen or seventeen, when I read *Gone with the Wind* three times in span of two summer months!!!

Margaret Mitchell, a privileged human whose life was cut short by a freak accident, immortalized an era, historically, politically, and geographically, by weaving a story through the life of an ambitious young girl. She was not too dissimilar to Scarlett in ambition, although she was lucky in a sense and went in better direction.

Shy of five foot with a vast spirit-engulfing love of literature and sensuality that was bordering on too liberal for her time, Mitchell generously offered her insight to us.

We visited her residence, "The Dump," now a museum. It was a delight to behold in Atlanta, which lacks charm but has a history steeped in racism. The ashes are still in the air as if the scars of the era are not removable.

Having been adventurous, Margaret Mitchell gives us a warning for charming psychopaths and their total lack of ability to make meaningful relationship. Rhett Butler seemingly pursuing a much younger lost girl, never appreciated the sincere love of a Madam whose house he frequented.

In a historical church, one of the few called the "First Church for Blacks," we were told of the plight of enslaved African-Americans through the "Underground Railway," a complicated system of secret messaging and safe houses owned by whites and Blacks to let the Blacks leave their harsh circumstances and, inch by inch, mostly at night, make their exodus from Atlanta to a few free states and Canada. Margaret Mitchell would have been very happy to learn that her book contributed greatly in informing the world about this dark state in her country.

Maybe a trace of charm in Atlanta was centred in the Martin Luther King Jr. story. Privileged by parentage and an availability of education, his sweet spirit was meant to liberate thousands who were tightly shackled by socially sanctioned ignorance, greed, and cruelty.

We also visited the original company manufacturing Coca-Cola. Late in the nineteenth century, a pharmacist named Dr. Pemberton made an energy drink of cocaine and caffeine and eventually made a fortune from it. They had to remove the cocaine later.

Savannah was all charm and intrigue and had a serious dark side. Today, it's a humble city with a prosperous colonial past, lying along the Savannah River. With all the imports coming in, where fictional Rhett Butler would buy his luxurious items for his favourite ladies or corrupt politicians.

It's ornamented by old, old southern oaks and palms, with a multitude of green, leafy squares named after one or another industrialist or war hero. The city is small, not vulgar like NYC, not formidable like Chicago, nor short of oxygen like Atlanta. The affluent streets still have relics of genius pavements made by a mixture of oyster shells, salt, and sand. These pavements are indestructible. Alas, most were replaced by fashionable bricks and asphalt.

In their stately houses with ornate statues and banisters, one hears of more than one murder in the years past. The most infamous one is the mysterious disappearance of a dreamer of a young man who befriended a rich bachelor antic dealer with impeccable taste not only for objets d'art but for young men. The book *Midnight in the Garden of Good and Evil* is about the story behind the murder trial.

In the most touristic area in Savannah, there is the statue of a life-sized girl holding two plates for birds to bathe in. It's called Little Wendy or Bird Girl and is originally the property of a family who placed it in Bonaventure Cemetery. After *Midnight in the Garden of Good and Evil* brought droves of tourists to Savannah, trampling statues all over, it was removed to a museum. The replica of it in all sizes can be purchased all over Savannah.

John Mercer, whose lyrics for "Moon River" vibrate with *The Adventures of Huckleberry Finn* penned by Mark Twain is a darling for the city. He apparently comes from one of the stately houses where a family member was murdered.

The whole experience was far grander from me being sixteen and mesmerized by Margaret Mitchell's South. And yet it could not be any closer to the core thanks to her keen eyes and pen.

MIXED BLESSING!

Friendships, like other blessings in life, have to go through many unfoldings and litmus tests. Unlike naked Archimedes's cry of "Eureka!" sometimes the discovery of the depth of friendship may point to a negative conclusion, yet be enlightening, a blessing in disguise. The fact that it may not be pure gold saves us from unnecessary and at times harmful emotional investments. Although eventually all blessings prove to be of a mixed nature. Life is rife with paradox.

Fair-weather friends have their own beauty. We can have lots of fun for a limited time, even on a repeated basis, but we can never share our vulnerabilities and sorrows without compromising our integrity. Just because we are going through a loss or have met a misfortune, it does not mean we like to be pitied. We only want to have a witness for our experience the same way we want to share our happiness without being envied.

This need for having a witness in our life is tightly intertwined with our need for personal space. One cannot be without the other.

A few years ago, in an extra-cold winter, with a fair-weather friend, a witness to experience fun with, I enjoyed a lovely opera by Puccini. The centre offers the best of operas, ballets, and other performances of a classical nature to refined audiences, which is more and more an elite group due to hefty ticket prices. It's located in downtown Toronto, central to business, enriched by substantial, solid buildings that are home to many icons of success.

And, not surprisingly, it's a hub for homelessness.

The opera finished close to 9 p.m. after a generous standing ovation for a well-presented performance of the tragic life of a young, hopeful human. Like most operas it was a tragic story. This one saw a Japanese woman losing her hope and child to an entitled American who had impregnated her. These melodically impressive experiences are a form of witnessing life's paradoxes, an intense, consuming love ending so badly. That's why we see them over and over again and they never lose their original effect (my dear Mozart, your delightful operas, even "Don Giovanni," are not tragic, just cautionary tales).

My fair-weather friend always wants to go for a dessert and decaf coffee after a performance. I like to continue the fun, but on this winter night, dark and frozen, I had to succumb to her overriding enthusiasm, which I didn't quite share. By the time our laughter-filled light conversation finished and we said farewell, it was close to midnight. I had to walk five minutes to reach my car in a nearby indoor parking lot.

Toronto City Hall, lighted and colourful, was across Queen Street. I was walking along its east side edging onto Bay Street, which was still noisy with traffic splashing thawed ice. I had to be very careful not to slip, negotiating each step on the hard ice on the pavement, my eyes fixed on the ground.

In my intense self-preservative state, I noticed colourful objects along the way. I looked to my right along Bay Street, and saw close to a dozen makeshift beds set back from the sidewalk. Neatly arranged in a row, some distance from each other, were homeless men in deep sleep. They were tucked into their covers as if a loving hand had done it. They were from young to middle aged.

My heart ached. These men were loved babies once. Each one could be my father, uncle, brother, husband, son, friend. I knew shelters are open for them. I had read that concerned taxpayers of Toronto had even reserved good number of rooms in a hotel for those reluctant to go to s shelter. Yet my heart was aching badly, painfully.

But wait.

They were in a deep sleep, on Cruel Street, in the freezing winter, with the blaring light from city hall and the screeching splashing sounds of traffic. They were deeply asleep, having voluntary fellow witnesses experiencing the same, trusting each other with their personal space. They looked so dignified. They had their way.

Puccini, in his other opera, was helping me to see another paradox, a mixed blessing, as in my mind, I was hearing the victory aria, "Nessum Dorma," with a chorus "Vincero," coming from the row of beds, as I was walking away. They had refused to have fair-weather friends.

I was going to my home in the suburbs, quiet and serene, to a comfortable bed, warm and cozy, to suffer my chronic insomnia and interrupted sleep.

PARENTHOOD, THE MOST ENLIGHTENING EDUCATION

For me, parenthood was the toughest and most enlightening unknown.

I became a mother shortly after becoming a psychiatrist. All along, I had thought that I would not be qualified to be a mother without such an education. It was proved to be a false notion, the product of the mind of a five-year-old. Only much later did I realize that all my education only brought me to the entry level of the highest education called parenthood.

Parenthood was a realm completely alien to the discipline of psychiatry. Indeed, I was most inept and uneducated in motherhood. My love for our children, however, compensated to a large extent for my ignorance. Not knowing, however, has been always exciting for me. There are still things to learn.

As our children grew and became more verbal, I had to hear a lot "You talk like a psychiatrist, not a mother!" I would feel crushed as I never used psychiatric jargon, even in my practice. They were referring to my poor vernacular tongue. Even in Farsi, vernacular was not my forte. Literary speaking had become my mother tongue.

On countless occasions, the mere transparency of our children clearly indicated that they knew English was not my mother tongue but I never wanted to use anything as an excuse for distorted communication.

I started to learn a new language by reading to them.

One of my most favourite authors was Charles Schulz, who condensed his understanding of life through the wisdom of Charlie Brown in comic panels. The language was simple, fluid, and quickly came to a meaningful point. In one episode, Charlie Brown's little sister, Lucy, insists that he read her a story. He is tired of reading to her, so he makes up the following while pretending to read from a book: "A man was born. He lived, and died. The end." Lucy, who was enraptured by the story, says, "What a fascinating story! Almost makes you wish you knew the fellow."

I was completely taken by his writing. I started to use my curiosity to enjoy the clarity of life rather than try to solve its riddles.

My parents had tried hard to discharge their parental responsibilities by encouraging education and virtuosity in us. They recited Socrates and Aristotle, and a doctrine for achieving a happy life by pursuing moral virtues. And yet the bedtime stories were about the city mouse visiting the country mouse, or Miss Beatle deciding to get married. They were simple parents to us. They were made happy by little things, and fought fiercely over nothing. They always gave me a feeling that the spirit of childhood was very alive in them. At "The end," their lives became fascinating stories. Completely unharmed by their philosophy.

My gratitude toward them became evermore as I kept navigating and improvising in motherhood and realizing that they had also improvised a lot with us.

I relented from living a virtuous life in pursuit of happiness. I became a student of Charlie Brown. I wanted my life to be a fascinating story. I wanted to feel ordinary as much as possible. I have accomplished two stages of it by now. The third for sure I will accomplish someday. But for the moment, I am in the entry stage of being a grandmother and am intensely enjoying the pleasure of knowing nothing again. For my grandchildren, just like for my children, I am that grandma who could not speak English. All this progress I owe to my children and the gift of motherhood which my loving parents cultivated in me. It seems that parenthood was the toughest and most enlightening education for me.

She Got Me First and Brought Me to My Senses

I had just finished a long, generous visit with my sister, and was ready to enter my own meditative state, when a lady entered my room and, after a few seconds of tentative staring, she said, "My name is Emilia. I am a volunteer who listens to patients who need to talk to somebody." Her formal tag verified her introduction. "What is your name?" she asked me.

She was tall and statuesque, in her sixties or more, and stylishly and meticulously dressed. Her straight, shoulder-length greyish-blonde hair neatly framed her impassive face. Her blue eyes pierced through her sparkling glasses. I was comparing us. My reading glasses always have smudges. And I was in my most disheveled rehab style.

It was the third week after a reconstructive surgery on my left upper tibia, which had been shattered to pieces by a careless driver while I was crossing the street.

I had got the best medical care and was instructed by my brave, loving surgeon of three months not to put any weight on my left leg—hence, the lengthy rehab.

I was most courteous with Emilia while expressing zero interest in a chat.

But her eyes became more transfixed on mine and she kept questioning me about me and I obliged, again demonstrating zero interest.

Two thoughts were parading through my mind: one, why she is not getting it? The other one, she is going to have varicose veins with that rigid posture.

Finally, in her persistent, intrusive, albeit very polite, questioning, she arrived at asking my profession and again I obliged.

Suddenly, her transfixed gaze became fluid and communicative with my eyes and she said, "Oh! I have schizophrenia!" As if she had finally overcome all my deliberate refusal to connect with her, and had baited me from the depths of my internal quagmire to a more humane form.

She had met the potential soulmate in me from the first moment, long before I had gotten her.

I gave her my most sincere praise for having cooperated with her treatment and for being so beautifully functional. She said she had fought with the diagnosis for ten years, and so had the psychiatrists! But she has been in great shape for forty years, once everybody accepted the condition.

We said a warm goodbye. And I thought to myself: Oh my god, I had never persisted so much to touch another soul, always fearing intrusion and harm.

Blame it on the Hippocratic oath—or, more accurately, my personal handicap.

But Emilia had an ability and license to do it. And she did it well.

She had very mild side effects from her medication, now I realized.

I felt immense gratitude to be part of a great health-care system and was flattered by our amazing community.

STORIES FROM REHAB

Those loving fingers.

Among my fellow injured there were people who were burned accidentally in household accidents.

I am sitting beside one today, in the OT room.

A large man with smiling blue eyes. Somebody one could imagine always saying jokes and sanitizing the environment by making people laugh.

He is in his thirties. We are all talking about our lives outside this room—our spouses, children, travels, and adventures. The best prescription to enhance hope.

His one-time lovely skin, from face and head to upper body and hands, has turned to some pink-brown colour, a shiny, elastic substance after plastic surgery.

The OT assistant, a young, fit woman, is working on his fingers, all too deformed and immobile, one joint at a time, with unfathomably caring attention, with dainty, skilled fingers.

Those fingers that will embrace her loving husband and squeeze the cheek of her toddler, after she leaves for home tonight.

He looks at me with his signature joyous eyes, now tormented by pain, cringing after each forced movement, and moans with pain and says, "God be my witness! I want to punch her in the face! I have great control though!"

She responds calmly, without taking her eyes from his fingers or stopping her work: "I know. It's so hard!"

He says, "And it's the only way." Now there's a twinkle in his eyes and a deep appreciation in his tone.

In Praise of Rehab: We All Can Rely on the Kindness of Strangers

Saying goodbye has always been difficult for me, in any form. I want to weasel out of it and a lot of time I succeed.

Now that I am leaving rehab, I feel almost nostalgic. I don't want to weasel out.

I learned, laughed, shared, experienced grief, anger, and disappointment, and developed kinship with many.

Who was that angel who patrolled my bed at midnight, and covered me nightly in my highly sedated state? I never saw her face in the daylight, but I always thought I had a glance of her while patrolling in the dark and saw the most beautiful life form.

When I inquired about her, I was told that her name was Kamil, that she was a recent graduate and could only get the night shift, in various wards.

The staff in rehab, aside from the medical group, were from a multitude of fields walking through the halls, rooms, and offices. An endless arrival of paramedics, and departures arranged by special vans whose drivers would come straight to the patients' rooms: housekeeping, mailmen, lab technicians. kitchen staff, volunteers, student nurses,

149

and ever-flowing visitors. And here, my iPhone, iPad, credit cards, ID, and cash were in complete exposure to all, even when I was absent from my room. I felt so safe. In Gare du Nord, Paris, where police infiltrate the station, in a split second, my handbag containing the aforementioned items, was snatched by Rembrandts in thievery! My fellow injured neighbour's husband, who brought me coffee and *The Toronto Star*, and later on shyly put the most delicious samosa on my table, will not be forgotten.

The animated occupational therapist who encouraged a lively environment for fellow injured souls will be missed.

The housekeeping lady with an elaborate hair-do and fresh perfume would not be giving me a smile on her shift anymore.

The volunteers would not bring my meals, freshly made in the rehab kitchen based on a recommended balanced diet.

The twenty-one-year-old motorcyclist with multiple injuries will not exchange jokes during our physiotherapy time.

No longer for the third time the ultra-polite frustrated voice on the speaker will invite visitors to leave, as it's 9 p.m., and visiting hours ended at 8:30.

I have developed immense respect for our health-care system and the people who deliver it, who are its most important representatives.

I could not be in a private room because their priority goes to critical cases.

My understanding of courtesy, tolerance, and goodwill has exponentially deepened.

I resumed knitting after decades and my daughters-in-law were most gracious to accept my amateurish products for their children.

My friends visiting me in rehab expressed their joy for my staying seated and not running around to dote on them the way I host people at home.

In rehab I was put in a situation where I was forced to accept kindness from strangers, friends, and family.

Oh my God, it's so delicious to be a recipient with no chance for reciprocation!

PAIN IS OUR
BEST FRIEND

"So, your body is too painful all over. Where does it hurt most?" One of the two lawyers addressed me on the manicured grounds of rehab, a place that was chosen by the legal team, including a law clerk, to start the legal dialogue.

I was in my wheelchair, my left leg in a black removable cast called a "zimmer," stretched forward. "I am completely pain-free," I responded.

One could not imagine the fearful disbelief in their faces, as if we were surrounded by the insurance company's detectives behind every tree and flowering bush.

He said hurriedly, "Of course! You are maxed out on painkillers."

Me: "I have not taken any painkiller since a week after my operation."

Now one can imagine how we were escalating toward a communication breakdown.

Pain is the bread and butter of an injury lawsuit. They felt empty-handed with a totally uncooperative client.

It did not matter that I had lost a part of my body and all its precious functions. That I had lost my intactness. Bilateral oedema of ankles and numbing of sensory function were neither here nor there. That my joyous walks, hikes, prancing about, over-the-shoulder rides for my grandchildren, bending backward and forward to feed them while pushing their strollers—all had come to an end.

All is time sensitive. I can't say I'll do it later. Soon, my grandkids would be too heavy to carry and no longer in a stroller.

It did not matter that soon I would develop an arthritic condition in my wrists, elbows, and right hip as a result of pressure inflicted upon them by hopping.

I must have pain! Unbearable pain that forces me to take strong daily painkillers!

The fact that the left knee was not used at all and therefore the excruciating pain by putting pressure on it was yet absent, made no sense. The collateral losses of pleasure and exhilarating experiences did not count.

I came with a solution: I managed my pain by meditation.

Not good enough. The solid evidence was prescribed strong painkillers!

The lifesaving morphine injection, which stopped my shakes after the injury would be eternally appreciated and I'd beg for it if under similar circumstances again, yet I have encouraged everybody around me to manage their pain with willpower.

My babies so easily accepted that Mom's kiss takes all pains away. I have never prescribed painkillers or narcotics, despite a demand for them.

Yet I have always respected pain and considered it a great way for the body to communicate to us that something has gone wrong. My motto is: "Pain is my best friend!"

I won't have it as an enemy that has to be eradicated. In attempting to numb the pain I am not only blinding myself but damaging my body with unnecessary painkillers. I listened to my good friend who warned me what was going on and then I hoped to manage the wrong. At present, it's healing a repaired upper tibia and meniscus. I won't put any pressure on them for the next few weeks.

It just dawned on me that pain is considered a friend, albeit with different capacities, in other fields, too!

Piece of Cake . . .
Learning to Walk

Among other uncomplimentary traits inhabiting my personality, greed is prominent.

Fortunately, it has been limited to my own expectations and personal efforts, and its thrill overrides the exhaustion necessary for its fulfillment. Hiking and walking are activities that push the limit of my greed. The most common medium, however, is time. I just keep packing it up and stretching its seams until they inevitably come apart.

After a year of enjoying the Bruce Trail and Niagara Escarpment, discovered through hearsay, my horizon expanded and I embarked on my first hiking tour in Thailand. The tame terrains of Ontario were replaced with actually climbing steep hills and walking on paths barely one foot wide while looking down on deep bamboo forest ravines and valleys. I had not opted for any life-endangering experience. Indeed, the name of the tour company was "Comfortable Hiking," emphasizing *safe* and *easy*, targeting seniors.

Many of the tour members were in their late sixties and some well into their seventies. These were very strongly built men and women with extensive biking, canoeing, and hiking histories. I was a complete novice with practically no hard experience and, worse, I was totally uninformed of inherent risks. I just loved hiking.

Each time I faced a long, steep hill, I felt silently shaky inside, thinking there was no chance I could make it. And right at that moment, one of our tour mates, a tall, slim gentleman who was clearly much older than me, looking at the same spectacle, would say, "Piece of cake!"

That worked like a silky spur on my stalled body. A piece of cake for him? Wow! And before I knew it, I was halfway ahead. My speed only revealed my lack of experience to these highly seasoned hikers with bodies built far more strongly than mine. I frequently thought he'd read my mind and was trying to encourage me.

With each tour I learned about more fascinating places and greedily expanded my fun, which at times due to my sheer lack of knowledge became more and more life-endangering, taking a lot of the fun out of the experience. But each time, the limit of possibilities was pushed further.

As I approach the date I can finally put my left leg down on the ground, I anticipate something unpleasantly unfamiliar. I don't have any memory of how I started and learned to walk as a toddler. The injury caused by a car accident demands retraining.

To have a rehearsal, a few days ago, I replaced my walker with two elbow crutches and, without putting any weight on my left leg, tried to maintain my balance. A sense of dread took me over. Tears welled up in my eyes and streamed down my face. I could not possibly do it. My nervous system was not registering a left leg as a functional member. The emerald-green vertical hills of Machu Picchu were quite doable compared with this.

Suddenly, the image of the tall gentleman in Thailand appeared in my retreated mind. With his keen eyes fixed on a long, steep hill, he was saying, "Piece of cake!"

This piece of cake, relearning to walk, had to be enjoyed and mastered with great patience, the same way he walked up the steep hill. Not my hurried way. Now I feel he was actually encouraging himself. But it worked like a charm on me, too. I just had to harness my greed.

STORIES FROM REHAB: BRAVE TO LEAVE

In my occupational therapy session, I met a wiry, spritely, lively lady, well into her eighties, whose pretty face was undaunted by the fog of age. She talked loudly about her adventurous tours and her specific love for canoeing. She was working on strengthening her hands. Both with obvious reduced strength. She was convincing the occupational therapist that nothing had been achieved by therapy, that it had all been about her own practice, and that time had been an important factor. The occupational therapist was very frustrated but kept her smile as she attributed all the improvement to the therapy and insisted she still needed it.

She won! She coerced her will to be discharged so she could travel in two weeks to Romania with her old hiking group.

At one point, our eyes met and she asked me about my accident. Then I asked her about hers.

She said she was a hiker and canoeing expert and that when they were in Mongolia a few months before, they experienced a head-on collision car accident and she had been left with a broken jaw and broken shoulders and arms!

My God, these surgeons perform miracles!

But I also thought she was the spirit of a miracle. She knew she couldn't canoe or even hike ten kilometres a day in her condition. But she knew that being where she loved to be and with people she had enjoyed for decades was the fastest way to recovery.

She gave me so much inspiration. I could not take the smothering of all those kind souls who wanted to watch me recover.

My recovery was going to happen outside of rehab.

And I was rushed to recovery by being soaked in love by those close to my heart.

I Got Plenty
o' Nuttin'! In a
Multifaceted Area

Gershwin is a latecomer in my musical lexicon, but ever since I heard "American Rhapsody in Blue," for some reason, Mozart showed up in my mind Google. Indeed, whenever I thought of Gershwin, Mozart appeared. And gradually the monitor of consciousness became dotted with more. Then I realized many beautiful melodies, such as "Summertime," "I Got Rhythm," and "Someone to Watch over Me" had been his compositions. So maybe his music had been in my data long before I knew his name. Just like Mozart's.

How could this loutish rascal from the rough streets of dirty New York in the very early twentieth century, illiterate and musically ignorant, blossom into such an eternal flower in the musical garden by age fifteen? Receiving his first musical lesson around age twelve, he was multi-talented in other areas as well, all with little or no training.

Mozart, over a hundred years earlier, had been soaked in music genetically, and received a hothouse form of training in an educated, affluent family. He, however, maintained his originality by acting as a rascal. Yet the music of both is defined as innocent and honest.

Ray Charles's instrument was his larynx, and he brought his genre of innocent tunes to our parched ears. He was doted on by his teenage single mother, who worked as a washer woman. Her singular focus was to make her boy self-sufficient—in particular, after he lost his eyesight by age seven. Trained in classical music in a school for the deaf and blind, Charles used his vocal gifts to enchant us. Being blind at such a young age spared him from feeling different as a Black man. His music attracted all. Although his near-instant colossal success became a slippery road toward a few decades of heroin addiction. But his own personal strength and determination freed him to share his gift for many years to come. I consider "You Don't Know Me" a song that represents his inner beauty. He grabbed all the contemporary tunes and made his own genre of soul music. Ray Charles was carrying a torch for the emancipation of his country from racism without a noise but his vocal impressions.

"Whenever I see a beautiful thing, I steal it. Good artists copy, great artists steal," was Picasso's answer to his critics who thought many of his artistic creations were not original. Not plagiarism. But discerning eyes can notice similarities in the DNA of Picasso's art compared to earlier original artworks. In a way, Picasso, despite his psychological glitches, helped freedom of expression for painters. So innocent and honest. Picasso, despite his millions, had to live poor to shine the treasure of his talent out of the ore of life's absurdities.

Creation by humans means appreciation of their creator. Grabbing all the beauties around and giving them a personal touch. Taking wings from inner restraint in a highly self-disciplined way.

In musical parlance, Bach is the DNA of music and smart musicians spawn self-expression pivoted around his sentences.

Gershwin's "Porgy and Bess" is the story of the plight of Blacks from the tyranny of racism in the southern slums of the U.S., a perennial blight as real as the hurricanes. Without acting as a hero, Gershwin's music played a part in awakening social consciousness in Americans. No utopia anywhere, just daring to take one step at a time.

Gershwin had received mainly disapproval from his classical fellows. But "Porgy" brought him an onslaught of social dissent. His courage was not forged by a militant soul. Just by experiencing a wealth of nothingness.

Gershwin was not dissimilar to Shakespeare; whose lack of university education caused his literate contemporaries to treat him with arrogance brewed in ignorance. And his depiction of universal truths brought him disdain from the elite attached to their established norms. Shakespeare also stole great stories and re-immortalized them.

The lyrics of "Porgy and Bess" are in the language of the Black slum. In the aria "I Got Plenty o' Nuttin'," Porgy, a disabled street beggar in love with Bess, declares his happiness for being in love and having stars in the sky for free and being connected to all blessings.

Gershwin died young like Mozart, but lived a life filled with activities longer than 100 years. And, like Mozart, he will live for many hundreds of years more.

I have a feeling that all these contributions to life's beauty let themselves experience the wealth of having nothing.

I like to identify with Porgy by stealing his line and removing it from the slum: "I got plenty of nothing," in just appreciating all the beautiful things that come my way.

STORIES FROM REHAB: FIRST STEP TOWARD CIVILIZATION

As I am re-emerging into the world of the majority, my self-consciousness about my appearance is getting heightened. How do I look to others? I ask myself. I am injured and have felt entitled to be disheveled. But now on this early Sunday morning being escorted on my walker, hopping toward the physiotherapy room for the first time, I am suddenly gripped by other people's impressions of me. I ask the recently graduated physiotherapist assistant shimmering with the brilliance of youth, who is escorting me, "What is the etiquette in rehab regarding appearance? Like, should we be dressed nicely? Wear make-up? Have neat hair? Smell good?"

She says that for her, smell is important. And I think of her, just past twenty, enjoying the heavenly scent of youth, and I am happy that I'm not ruining it by not having used commercial perfume.

She has already interfered with her impeccable young face by using totally unnecessary eyeliner. She continues: "I notice old ladies here worry a lot about their hair."

I go back in time to my pubescent years, which were governed by a mind as sophisticated as a three-year-old, when my mother would repeatedly look at me with great concern and say, "All you need is a bit of pink on your cheeks and lips." And then try to apply her rouge on me and I would wipe it off and run away.

I looked like an emaciated little girl with sallow skin, and had a nickname of "Yellow" after two long-term tropical illnesses around age five. And then at puberty I was transformed to a chubby adolescent. My mother's remedy for making me presentable, however, was relentless: "Just some pink over your cheeks and on your lips." As she faced my resistance at any intervention, she became more elaborate in her reasoning. Her final and oft-repeated one was: "Beautification is the first step toward civilization. It means you care for other people. You don't want people to suffer by looking at you. And all you need is some pink!"

A few years later, I was beyond civilization, selfishly applying multiple lotions and potions and colours to create a masked face for the suffering public.

Now in rehab, I really wanted just to be civilized, caring not to offend others with my sight. I wished for the days when only some pink would suffice and for my mother's concern and honest impression of me. I know she was right because whenever I look at my daughter I want to say, "Please don't interfere with your natural beauty." She does not need even a bit of pink. But I want her to observe the first step toward civilization: beautifying herself.

In my present form, I have a few treacherous steps to take. It feels more like hopping on one foot. Still far from trying to be civilized.

THREE HOTS
AND A COT

The whole of Australia is a long, circular oceanfront. I've been told that the vast internal land does not appeal to people. Maybe only some Aboriginals, unaware of the region's recent past history go there.

My friend and I had been in a congress set in sunny, white, modern, flowery Melbourne, divided by Yarrow (ever-flowing) River, strewn by native arts, large and small. One gets the impression that Australian settlers had amended and continued to amend and repent the bad behaviour of their ancestors toward Aboriginals.

We were under the impression that kangaroos ran freely in Australia but, alas, we scarcely saw them, even in a major zoo. Eucalyptus trees, with their blue hue and strong, pungent scent, however, were as abundant as olive trees in Corfu.

Australians are generally friendly and relaxed, but they never rush to touch you all over like their flies. It was shortly before Christmas and the land was blessed with warm, bright sunshine. We were told that, due to the very hot, dry weather of the season, flies were searching for humidity through humans, mostly their facial orifices. But they were harmless.

In an older downtown area, there were attractive shopping streets decorated with Christmas trees and ornaments. For those living in Canada, it was so interesting to see Christmas in a green summer climate. We had taken a short lunch-hour to visit this area. In the beautiful square, a TV crew was approaching passersby and asking about their Christmas traditions, knowing a large number of them were tourists. We got their attention, too. After a short chat, I said to the interviewer, "I love your accent!" And he, as comfortable and easy as any Australian, responded softly, "I don't have an accent. *You* have an accent!" We laughed and said Merry Christmas.

We had planned an after-conference tour to Sydney, so beautiful and sun-soaked.

We had several sightseeing tours by bus and, during one ride, I noticed a sign for Bondi Beach.

Bondi Beach, in the vicinity of Sydney, attracts tourists as much as the Sydney Opera House, if not more.

I, however, had no prior knowledge of it. On the spur of the moment, I decided to visit it.

My friend had no interest, so I took a local bus early in the morning to go there. It was mid-morning when I arrived. Bondi Beach was massive and welcoming. Surfers were all over the blue Pacific waves emitting silver foam, and people were stretched out and relaxed on the sand.

I chose a spot to sit and just watch the happiness around me when I noticed a tall, slight gentleman in his seventies approaching me with his surfboard. He said hello and asked if he could sit near me. I welcomed him and, within a few minutes, he was telling me his story.

He lived in one of the apartment buildings surrounding the beach, a retirement place for army veterans. He had no family and he passed his days visiting the beach, surfing, and swimming, and his evenings with friends and neighbours having fun. Drinking is a pastime in Australia, but not like Ireland or Scotland.

As a young man starting life with no skills or a trade, he found going into the army the easiest way to have "three hots and a cot"—food and shelter. He received excellent training to kill the enemy and protect himself. One aspect of field training over an extended period was in a central area of the land, where the British were conducting nuclear experimentation at the service of weaponry for war.

His service in active war was short. But upon the calming down of war season, he and his surviving comrades were called for a gathering. There, they were told that what they were going to hear must never be transferred to any outsider. Those young men in their early twenties were told that nuclear radiation had most probably caused some harmful mutations in their reproductive organs and that they therefore must never have offspring. For their loyalty they would be granted secure housing and income. In other words, lifelong three hots and a cot.

He told me this story because the time he had to keep the secret had lapsed and now he was allowed to talk about it. The British had abandoned the field and most people did not know about existing nuclear waste. He was happy with his life on the oceanfront.

I was not sure if it was a simple coincidence that he spotted me among many others or if, somehow, he spotted someone so far away that he felt it would be easy to break his long-held silence. I did not question if he thought the price for a lifelong three hots and a cot was worth it.

That evening, back at the hotel, my friend was so intrigued by my description of Bondi Beach that she wanted us to go there the next morning, fourteen hours before our flight to Hong Kong. Wow! That's my way of cherishing the gift of time. Use every minute.

We put our suitcases with the concierge of the hotel and, after a brisk walk, took a nice, airy bus ride with a few passengers. As we walked out of the bus, I felt so light and joyous in the crisp, warm, golden morning, the blue Pacific rhythmically pulling itself forward, offering shiny layers of silver as if welcoming us. I stretched my hands toward the ocean and felt too light! There was no burden on me. I had left my little handbag containing my ticket, passport, and all my cards and cash, on the bus.

The blue of the water, the gold of the sun, the clear, blue, cloudless sky, the white sand, and the ambiance of beachgoers were replaced by a whole-morning interaction with Australian police, who unanimously reassured me that my handbag would be retrieved.

There are strict laws in Australia to respect and protect tourists, as tourism is a major source of their revenue. My bag was found and we got on the plane. But my poor handbag and I were fated to part in future mishaps.

Did my friend ever see Bondi Beach on that day or will her memory be confined to my description of it the day before?

BEWARE THE
BLOODSHED

I witnessed the manic jubilation of Zimbabweans as they forced out their president, celebrating the end of a dictatorship and human rights violator. But what utopian regime would replace it?

Robert Mugabe, in the late 1980s, was considered the liberator of this cultured, prosperous, ancient country with the nickname "Jewel of Africa," which had lost itself first to the Portuguese and later to the British tyrant-colonizer Cecil Rhodes (the same man who tried to buy a good name by giving scholarships). Indeed, its name was converted to Rhodesia. Robert Mugabe was one of those who had liberated Zimbabwe from the reign of a white minority.

It is a déjà vu. For me, a totally apolitical person with no sense of history, what happened to Iran in 1979 was like a mixture of an earthquake, volcano, hurricane, and typhoon. And I do believe natural disasters, including climate change, are part of celestial management far beyond human intellect or control.

So, the unfathomable changes in 1979 were beyond the comprehension of those who were so eagerly looking for a change, the replacement of a tyrant, a puppet moved by Western power.

The winds of love and marriage had fixed me here. Never for a second had I contemplated leaving Iran. And learning about North America had made Iran far more dear in my heart.

In Canada, I had met rare Iranian students, as most Iranians went to the U.S. for continuing education. Most came from my neck of the woods, and were among the affluent, cultured, intellectual—i.e., apolitical—layer. Yet their reaction to upcoming change and a promised utopia was anticipatory excitement. Some change was better than no change.

But changes were happening in Iran: slow, sustainable, and progressive.

Our last house in Tehran was in a newly developed obscure suburb on the northern side of the city. Tehran was expanding constantly, affluence heading northward, poverty heading southward. Our house was close to a military base. Many mornings at the crack of dawn we were awoken by the sound of bullets, which meant some men—mostly young, suspected of being against the Shah—were executed. It was the sound of a faraway tragedy—until my own brother was imprisoned three times at the age of nineteen.

A very lively teen in need of some excitement, he had attended the never-ending, not-so-secretive rallies against the Shah, promising all young men like him that they might become the future king! My brother could have easily been the one whose execution at dawn would have woken us up. Good luck and a clean family history saved him. He got his PhD in social sciences from the University of Toronto, years later.

Even with such an experience, which shook our foundation, we believed the situation was getting better. Queen Farah, at a very young age, genuinely wanted her name to stay alive in history as a good queen who did a lot for her nation. And she did do a lot. The Shah, after a tragic forced separation from his first two wives, dictated by those who wanted pure Iranian blood for an heir, was becoming more secure. The paranoia that had been such a part of our nation was being replaced by optimism. Less prosecution and execution. Far more accountability and transparency.

So, I was dismayed by the happiness of my twenty-something expatriates. We were from a free, secular nation, had received top-notch university education for free, and freely had left to see the world in the latter part of our education.

Why were they happy while I was not, by the prospect of change? I had not listened to the audiotapes that were supposed to be by Khomeini, recited by a man in his forties and with some education, promising free houses for every Iranian and a share of the nation's oil and natural resources.

When my esteemed friends saw Khomeini in daylight and listened to his voice, which was devoid of intellect and education, they felt like fools. Where had this old, bearded man with a conspicuous turban been for the last fifteen or twenty years? He was supposed to be in jail or executed over political opposition but under the disguise of exile he had been kept safely in France. He was as safe in France as criminal money in Switzerland.

Who concocted the audiotapes? That shock was nothing compared with the emotional, intellectual, and spiritual concussion that came next. The bloodshed, multiplied summary executions, youth lost to war, paranoia and plundering of national resources had reached a historic pinnacle. The monarchy was dead. Viva bondage to the supreme dictator.

A few years ago, I was in South Africa, which was under the presidency of Zuma. Newly liberated from a century-long tyranny of the Dutch and, later, British exploitation, this African nation had enjoyed their first president, the beloved Nelson Mandela, who had been imprisoned for twenty-seven years.

The crime? Trying to prove that Blacks had no less intellect than whites. A video of a court event run on a perpetual loop in the Nelson Mandela Museum is tear-jerking. Dutch and British agents in the most sarcastic tones ask a young Mandela, a newly minted lawyer, "So, you are saying that a Black person has the same abilities as a White person?" And young Mandela, unphased and unoffended, responds,

"Yes. Given equal opportunity." He was condemned to life in prison for conspiring against the government.

He was elected to lead the country after his release. Mandela bowed out after five years of a balmy presidency, never leaving his humble lifestyle.

Zuma had spent ten years in the same famous Robben Island prison for being in the Communist party. Like most hardcore Communists, his taste for excess was boundless and he had pursued the presidency vehemently, and now was having the time of his life. Many wives and too many children, a mansion with a fortified fence, a larger-than-Olympic-sized pool, and a history of corruption charges, all at the expense of this ultra-resourceful country. He did not share much of his newly achieved wealth with his people.

But the majority of South Africans wanted to pay him his due for being ten years in prison and then he would go. They were not looking for a revolutionary change. They wanted to avoid carnage, continue slow national progress, and maintain hard-achieved stability.

And were the jubilant Zimbabweans ready for massive bloodshed? And increased chaos?

Well, when the blood belonged to others, young dreamers, innocent families totally uninvolved with power plays, then it was cheap. Iranians paid a lot and are still paying. Hopefully, there will be no more revolution, just slow, sustainable progress at the grassroots level, which is really the maker of the ruling party at any human society.

My heart goes out to the innocent Zimbabweans.

LOSS IN TRAVELLING: MASTER THIEVES IN PARIS

For decades, there have been signs in Paris and London alerting tourists about pickpockets. Oliver Twist was a fictional character based on the real craft, art, and science of thievery. The mecca of open-market thievery, however, is now in Paris. They are attributing it to a new genre of thief with a superior, innate aptitude that has introduced a new level of precision and teamwork to the craft.

It was my fourth time in Europe, visiting almost the same destinations, where I had frequented cities, towns, and villages on foot, as well as many of its taxis and underground stations. This journey was with my sister Vida, a seasoned traveller. We had compressed visiting many cities into a short time.

Our first destination was London, where we walked along the Thames with all its attractions: the Thames cruise, farmers' market, and the shrine they have made in Harrods for the tragic Diana. I have never understood why people visit Stonehenge, but we visited Emily Dickinson's house, now a cafe and museum, and the Roman ruins in Bath. The best Scottish pasty is made by a Czech family there.

We arrived at Gard du Nord of Paris, a busy hub for people arriving from the airport, and departures by various modes of transport. The din was dizzying, the loudspeakers constantly announcing departures, and the dome-shaped station was infiltrated by police officers.

We wanted to buy our next local trip ticket as well as underground tickets to our hotel. All was done in no time, and I transferred my francs from my carry-on to my handbag, the one I had lost in Tehran and later at Bondi Beach, where it was returned safely. This well-worn handbag was waterproof, small, but spacious, and had accompanied me in my hiking trips as well as other tours. It contained all my usual possessions, including my brand-new iPad. As we started to walk toward the exit to the underground, I put my handbag on my carry-on handle. In less than a minute, it was no longer there.

At first, we just looked around. There was no chance, with the heavy passenger traffic, to detect anything on the floor.

A police officer was standing within two steps. I went to him and said, "Sir, I lost my handbag." In clear English, he said, "Madame, you have not lost your handbag. It was stolen from you. And you'll never get it back!"

He was rather impatient with my disbelief and explained to me that gypsies are sanctioned by the French government and that nobody can catch them. By sanctioned, he meant that carding was illegal. If you have proof of their theft, bring it on. But nobody could catch them in the act.

Grudgingly, he took me to the police depot in the station, which dealt with lost and found and unruly conduct. During the hour I was there, I witnessed at least forty officers, men and women, enter and exit from a door next to the front desk, in the back of the tiny room. Each entrance and exit were accompanied by the police officer kissing the ones at the desk twice on the cheeks, in a reciprocal way. Even in my state of despair, I found that amusing. This insistence on creating a sense of community and trust was commendable. But it only caused delay for me.

All our plans had collapsed. To get an expedited passport from the Canadian consulate in Paris, with their sacred long hours for lunch and snacks, and given that it was Labour Day weekend in Canada, seemed absurd. It was Sunday. Our flight to Venice was on Tuesday.

After an hour and filling out lengthy forms, with persistent reassurance from the front-desk police that I'd never get my handbag back, we left.

Now my eyes were scanning people. I actually noticed this new genre of pickpockets, dressed as if in uniform and with fearless, smiling, distinct faces roaming Gard du Nord, and, later, all over Paris—mostly near hotels or places frequented by tourists. One picks with the speed of light and passes the object to the next, and the next and the next.

Once you are jaded, pickpockets don't bother with you because the delivery of their art and science depends on a guilelessness factor in the tourist. But I was approached by a girl four or five years old whose parents and siblings were spread around the hotel entrance, charging at my bagless self, knowing all would be in my pockets. I had nothing on me. The girl had a great future.

These Rembrandts of thievery could have used their IQ and talent doing a lot more. Such as making the atomic bomb? No! The French government may have a point.

Now Vida was my bank, phone, protector, and supporter, while I was in an emotional concussion. And yet we managed to walk along the Seine River and see tourist sites, and even have dinner at a boat restaurant on the water before we were hit by the evening cold of September.

The consulate was filled with Canadians being robbed in various ways and places. But being good sports, nobody was complaining. Despite the sacred croissant and coffee and lunchtime, with the total cooperation of the passport office in Canada, which had put posters all over the walls of this small space that they were open twenty-four hours to help Canadian citizens, my passport was issued on Wednesday.

Except for a deflated spirit and the loss of a considerable amount of money, I managed to see and enjoy our prearranged destinations. Maybe one condition for happiness is to have nothing to lose.

Once, I asked an obliging Frenchman, "Why do people come to Paris? It's grey and ugly and unsafe and yet they call it the city of lights." He said, "Paris is like a beautiful woman. She will hurt you when you get close to her."

In Venice, we were in an ancient, renovated hotel with beautiful Persian carpets, even in our room, courtesy of the hard times that had fallen on Iran.

In Pisa, we touched the leaning tower and ran to catch our train and escape a pickpocket who was approaching us as if she were a railway official, before going to Tuscany.

We enjoyed the azure of the Mediterranean all over. In Athens I was finally able to find the prison and the place where Socrates drank the hemlock rather than be hanged.

In the eye-caressing Greek island of Santorini, with little, pastel houses on the hilltops, in a restaurant on the Aegean Sea, my sister enjoyed the famous sunset. I was sheltering myself inside from the fierce winds, the same winds that had accompanied Ulysses on his odyssey, seriously endangering his life, as well as taken him home safely. That was a life with or without gypsies.

As fate would have it, I was destined to tremble far worse by another loss.

Multilayered Paradise

The pleasure I get from my grandchildren is far purer than what I felt with my children. I have no illusion that I can or want to shape them. With my children, I was burdened by a serious misunderstanding that, in some way, I was the architect of the edifice of their humanity.

And then every day, under my loving and keen observation, as I weighed them and measured their heights, and reviewed the words and concepts they had learned, the milestones they had passed and the tasks they had mastered, I also noticed they were becoming themselves. For a brief time, this accurate perception made me anxious to try harder to "shape them" and turned my efforts more vigorous and tiring. And soon the lightbulb went off: I was just a lucky presence in the Disney World of human development.

Just watch them grow. What a paradise. The paradise gets more expansive with grandchildren. The fear of making errors and not being on the favourable side does not apply in this relationship. Their smile when they recognize my presence sends me to the height of self-centredness. My God! How easy it is to make them happy.

Sometimes against their parents' wishes. An apricot gobbled by one of them tasting like metaphorical manna from heaven, before dinnertime, right at the exit from daycare, brings the same heavenly joy to me. They have zero expectation, an essential feature for personal happiness. We lose this precious asset during our development, but luckily, we can regain it with hard work.

No matter what I cook or prepare or give, their delighted faces delight me.

On Tuesdays, during good weather, I pick up my granddaughter Iris, not yet three, from daycare. I have usually prepared a four-course dinner for her, and sometimes five. Iris deliberates for a few seconds before acknowledging our connection. Then she looks at her caregiver, as if issuing my license to approach. And then the fun starts. She says something about her day as we walk to her stroller and wash her little hands with water from a bottle in preparation for dining.

From there, the stroller becomes a mobile restaurant, where Iris appreciates every bite and course while we simultaneously move toward one of the busiest beaches of Lake Ontario, just a few minutes south of the daycare.

Early in July, the blue of the sky and lake had joined seamlessly. The water was alive with gentle waves. Tree branches were dancing, touched by a pleasant breeze. Robins, cardinals, and chickadees were singing.

Along our way, I noticed a family was busy making use of a city designated barbecue spot not far from the beach. A delicious aroma spread in the air with each skyward cloud of white smoke.

Iris noticed the smoke and wanted us to halt near the barbecue, intensely looking at a young woman who was tending to multiple items on a little grill.

As Iris was still in the middle of her dinner—the third course—I suggested we sit at a nearby picnic table. Iris agreed. The stroller was parked. Iris kneeled on the bench to give herself a better view.

The woman was busy, as if in a delineated boundary like her own private kitchen, totally oblivious to passersby. Near the barbecue, a man her age in his swimming trunks was sitting on a large cloth mat spread on the grass, leaning on a maple tree and very busy Instagramming and talking into his phone. My first thought was: *So unusual! One always sees a man on the grill.*

As Iris's attention was not relenting, I suggested she walk toward the lady and talk to her. What I was doing? Was I shaping my granddaughter by encouraging her to be familiar with the world? But Iris did not heed me, though her inquisitive eyes remained fixed on the woman who was becoming speedier by the minute.

At this time, the man started to walk about and my earlier hunch was confirmed: he was actually talking to someone and using his phone to share a panoramic view of the surroundings: the lake, the barbecue, the trees and greenery. In a short while, he got close enough that I was able to get his attention by saying hello, and start a conversation.

He was kind enough to answer all my questions and more, which I presented as purely being due to Iris's interest!

They were from Romania. His wife, the queen of the kitchen, who by the way did not take her eyes off her responsibilities on the grill for one second, was making chicken, lamb, fish, and a lot more. Their four children were swimming, but arrived soon for dinner. I thought: How lovely that this man and woman had gotten married so young.

Upon arrival, the two tall teenagers started helping after changing and washing up by a large water container. The girl covered the nearby picnic table with a white embroidered tablecloth, and the boy brought over various items. White china dishes, plates and soup dishes were put in order, and cutlery enveloped by napkins appeared.

The motion of the lady at the grill had become frantic. She was dishing out items and mixing salad greens in a large bowl. Everybody was helping, including the younger boy and girl. And the king of the castle was proudly reporting on and Instagramming their delightful gathering.

All, just like me, seemed so appreciative of the health, beauty, and relative safety of the city, the country, the world at large in this little abode at that moment of time. Just a few kilometres away from the centre of Toronto, where we had stabbings and shootings on almost a daily basis.

All sat. Including Mom. And dining started. Better than any deluxe restaurant with that embroidered cloth table cover.

Iris, who had finished her third course and was now on her dessert of fresh fruit skewered in the style of shish kabobs (she loved the expression), had maintained her attention on the family—particularly the ones near her own age.

I looked around to see people lying tranquilly on the sand by the lake, or playing gleefully in the water, and children squealing and laughing, joyfully. Walkers were enjoying the beauty of the boardwalk in the receding sunshine. Bikers were safely riding in their designated bike lanes. Various boaters were enjoying the chance to be rowing in the water.

And my granddaughter now decided to approach the beach to play with the water.

The seagulls who were eagerly waiting for their morsels called out loudly for treats.

I felt in a multi-layered paradise.

CREATION AND EVOLUTION: THE ISLAND WITH SADDLED TURTLES

Once during a hike on the Bruce Trail, along the Grand River, I had the good fortune to be the random hiking buddy of a young mathematics professor. The hikers were from all walks of life, and their deepest conversations would be about nature and the history of the Niagara Escarpment, a terrain that was once deeply under water and ice, with a sharp, steep elevation of rocks. How had it happened? Volcanos, receding water, earthquakes? The young professor in the lightest language said, "In math, we know that 99 percent of problems in the universe cannot be solved." The weight that was taken from my shoulders by that sentence felt more like a metamorphosis, the shedding of one more obsolete shell. I had learned that nobody could answer the chicken-and-egg riddle. But other riddles just needed some thinking through.

On my own, however, thanks to long, passionate practice, I had come to the same conclusion as the young mathematician, but had never been convinced. One thing I was sure of was that the riddle considering genes versus environment was as absurd as pitting evolution against creation. Which sober mind, not even the crystal-clear one of the young mathematicians, would waste time seeing these as separate items? They are two perspectives that are so different and yet are inseparable and intertwined. Like a melody harmonized by two instruments.

With no interest or curiosity in seeing the Galápagos Islands, I found myself on a cruise navigating around the islands, and walking on those unique volcanic grounds. It happened to be in 2009, the centennial anniversary of the birth of Darwin, of whom I knew nothing except that he had tried to simplify the complexity of life.

One of Darwin's characteristics from early childhood was that he preferred the company of his own fabrication rather than learning from a bigger world. He failed practically everything before his parents shipped him to the Galápagos Islands. He was there only five weeks. Why does Darwin remind me of Christopher Columbus? They both were talented enough to weave elaborate fantasy around a speck of information.

There, he got access to valuable information recorded by Tomás de Berlanga in 1535, 300 years before Darwin arrived.

Father Tomas was named bishop of Panama by the Spanish Catholic Church. When going toward Peru, his ship was lost in a storm, and winds took him to an uninhabited island with a very unique habitat for interesting animals and plants. Father Tomas noticed that some of the gigantic turtles had shells very similar to horses' saddles; hence, he called it the island of saddled turtles: Galapagos. Being blessed with a keen power of observation, he made a painstaking study of all animals and plants and left the information on the island.

During his five-week stay on the island, Darwin put a finch to his own name and got access to Father Tomas's handwritten notes. He took them to England. It took him decades to find someone to write a book about his own ideas, including his famous evolution theory. In this regard, I think there is an uncanny similarity between Darwin and Thomas Edison, who got the benefit of Nikola Tesla's discoveries. Thank God for Elon Musk, who revived Tesla's name.

Cruising among large black volcanic rocks of immemorial time, and walking on black volcanic ground with traces of algae that's sprouted from it for 500,000 years, was like being transported in time. The terrain was studded by unique animals. And plants, all vulnerable to disappearance in a dry season, made me see creation all over, intertwined with evolution. One more sigh of relief. Another riddle I didn't have to think about, as my human brain did not have the app to comprehend it.

I enjoyed the jewel-like clusters of Sally lightfoot crabs with vibrant colours, sea lions defending their babies, iguanas leaving their droppings as a source of calcium for sea lions, pink and blue footed boobies, fish of many shapes and colours, even Darwin finch. The most memorable ones were little sally crabs sunbathing, resembling jewellery displayed on the black velvet of volcanic rocks, and their hasty retreat into the water.

We visited huge, solitary turtles with saddle-like shells, which at one time were the best food reservoir for pirates and mariners.

Earlier on, a hasty attempt to give more life to this uninhabited-looking island brought eucalyptus trees and goats to it, as both are hardy and proliferate rapidly. Now with more awareness about the utter fragility of this collective life form, any interference—including bringing food to the island—is prohibited. Goats are being shot by helicopter and eucalyptus trees have to be uprooted as they compete with limited food for endemic animals and plants. With some unwise intervention, both creation and evolution will stop. But does it? Never! Nature always starts from the end.

At the end of the journey I visited Quito, Ecuador, across the Pacific from Galapagos, a part of the world that enjoys lots of earthly symmetry, being right at the middle. The ancient Incan civilization, with European conquerors' footprints, is a world heritage site. It enjoys a location beside a river basin and at the foothill of the volcanic Andes. The architecture of this elevated city is interesting as houses have been built on the hill, requiring long, steep staircases.

Every few years, a major volcano blackens the houses and city with volcanic soot, and time and human effort clean it up. But the city is not in danger of disappearing by any interference.

Aged Love: Lovers in Limerick

A well-travelled and sociable colleague, Aghdas, kindly shared some trips with me. Considering that I snore terribly, she is a lucky sleeper. Once, we travelled to southern Ireland together. It was a first for both of us.

Like so many other European cities, four cities we visited were built along a lively, active river. And we walked them all and gathered memories around them. We were advised to carry umbrellas, but the frequent threat of rain happened to be just a short drizzle so I stopped carrying my umbrella, with clouds present at all times.

In Dublin, as soon as I made my usual "I am lost" face, a pair of the palest blue (courtesy of the scarce sunshine), kind eyes would be staring at me, and the kindest Irish voice—male or female—would ask, "Where would you like to go? May I help you?"

I had encountered this citizen alertness to tourists when I got lost in Hong Kong, where, without asking for help, locals offer it. A very busy place famous for the axiom: "Nobody can feel lonely in Hong Kong."

In Ireland, which is not all that busy, it felt that locals were going to help all the way.

Along River Liffey (Life), which is central to Dublin, such a person, a lady with laughter in her pale blue eyes, approached and wanted to help. We were looking for the bookstore/teahouse where readings

185

from James Joyce and Samuel Beckett were going on. Not that I had the slightest interest in touching any of their incomprehensible writing, which I had eagerly read in my less mature stage of being. It was just like wanting to look at London Eye with no intention of going for a ride again.

The lady was happy to tell us it was just along the way over the bridge. I noticed she lacked the sweet Irish accent. With more laughter, she said she'd lived for two years in the Annex neighbourhood of Toronto. And with us she tried to use her best Toronto accent!

Frequently, I tried to engage someone local to learn about leprechauns, but practically everybody avoided the subject in a shy way. I bought a leprechaun singing doll. I googled leprechauns but nothing stays in my mind. Maybe it's the essence of the leprechaun. Or maybe oral traditions work better for me.

My attempts to find a church to light candles were invariably met with a pair of pale blue eyes encouraging me to enter the one nearest me, and another lovingly wanting me to go just a few steps farther to another church. "Darling, this is a good Catholic church." "Love, why go to a Catholic church? There is a good Protestant church just over there." Or vice versa. There was no hostility for each other in their voices. Their differences were expressed politely and courageously. I went to both.

In Dublin, an owner of such pale blue eyes, a chubby young woman in ripped jeans (which became fashionable a few years later), who looked to be hooked on drugs, robbed my wallet from my zipped-up, tightly held handbag—of course in the train station. Locals had warned me about gypsies!

The word "pub" always rang risk, a drinking hole that I had only entered once by mistake in Toronto. "Pub" is synonymous with "restaurant" in Ireland. We frequented a lot of them for lunch and dinner, and witnessed copious volumes of beer being drunk by friends and family members without the slightest change in their public behaviour. At some places, the glasses were not picked up until after the patrons had paid and left. It felt like it was a badge of honour. The more, the better. Whiskey, the Irish water of divinity, required far more money. We were never given any attitude for not ordering a drink.

In Limerick, which is centred over the Shannon River, one Friday afternoon after a nice walk, Aghdas and I decided to eat dinner at a hotel restaurant/pub, an airy, glassed-in room with an informal setting and nice, low, upholstered seating arrangements. It was around 6:00 p.m., and the pub had just started to become vibrant with patrons and light. We chose a comfortable sofa with an oblong glass table. I was determined to try the famous aged Irish whiskey, despite the exorbitant price. The server explained how the water brings more divinity to this sacred, aged drink. It was wasted on me.

In the middle of our dinner, Aghdas nodded to my left and whispered, "I bet they are lovers."

Pretending the most natural glance around, I saw the couple. They were definitely of retirement age, with rather sturdy builds and nice clothes. They were sitting beside each other and their adjacent round glass table was already nearly full with their empty beer glasses. They were in a deep, intimate conversation. I said to Aghdas, "Yes. They are such lovers." Aghdas corrected me: "I meant they're having an affair. Married people have nothing to talk about." It was intriguing. Again, in my most skillful imitation of natural ways, I locked my eyes with their happy, pale blue eyes, and immediately said hello to trap them into a conversation.

They were retired, she as a social worker and he as a government employee, over forty years married, with grown children, and grandchildren, who came to this place every Friday. They lived nearby, just across the bridge. They made it politely clear that they wanted to save their precious seconds just talking to each other.

Having had lost our loving husbands in different ways, Aghdas and I had conveniently forgotten that love becomes more delicious with time. We were delighted at least to witness it in them.

Maybe there was some truth about sacred, aged Irish whiskey.

LOVERS' QUARREL RENEWAL OF WEDDING VOWS: MADNESS OF LOVE AT HOME

A simple lovers' tiff ended in a free-for-all, throwing objects from the second floor window, which was big enough to let a large, gilded wall mirror fly through it to the street. I was about seven years old when I witnessed every precious item in our living room being broken and finally the large gilded wall mirror being thrown from the window to the street below, where it shattered, loudly. All items were authentic dug antiques, at least 2,000 years old, wedding gifts from Maman's antique dealer and an excavator uncle.

My parents fought vigorously and violently to such an extent that we trembled seeing the seams of their marriage burst open just to release more passion to their relationship. During the nights of such fights—most nights—we witnessed our parents taking baths after they got over their parental responsibilities, Maman the last one to take a bath. And without any word available to our young brains, we knew of their conjugal bliss taking place, and thus of the safety of our parental roof being secured.

The fights were triggered by insignificant issues, but rooted basically and mostly by Maman's terrible anxiety of Baba joon marrying another woman. The intensity and solidity of this fear continued well into her seventies, until Baba joon passed away; it definitely had psychotic proportions.

This beautiful, educated, talented, totally against marriage woman, a principal of a co-ed school at age eighteen, a feminist for her own generation, had no sense of personal security.

Suddenly, at age twenty-two, she got anxious about her fertility and decided to say yes to the first gentleman caller. That victim was my father.

He was a dashing army officer but, at his core, he was a soft poet, of twenty-seven years. After being pursued by single and married women for a long time, he had met Maman's older sister, a pious, married woman of twenty-four, in Tehran. He had wished to marry a woman like her, so devoted to her husband with no attention to him. My future aunt indeed saw him the same way, a God-fearing man who was very respectful of her, and had wished him to marry one of her three younger sisters. My mother in her eyes was too strong and aggressive as she had secretly finished her high school at a time that good girls had accepted that to protect their virtues they must avoid education.

So, she tried to seduce my father to get interested in a sister who was perceived as soft and delicate. She points to her favourite sister's photo in the family photo album and says, "This one will be a lamb under your knife." Although she was really pretty, my father told me years later that the description of her character turned him off completely. He pointed at Maman's photo and my aunt said with an attitude, "She is principal of a co-ed school!" In today's parlance, this would sound like: "She is a lap dancer." My father instantly got smitten. He wanted a strong wife with great managerial aptitude.

The poor man travelled all the way to his birthplace, Arak, a small town southwest of Tehran, to ask for my mother's hand. And my mother, without asking any question about him, said YES. She had only one condition: She wanted to have the right to divorce if she was not happy with him.

He could not believe it. A girl must act fussy and reluctant. And nobody had ever heard of a woman having such a right. So, my father retreated! And came back fast. If she was thinking of divorce then marriage would not be a trap.

At their expedited wedding night when they retired to the special room with a dinner table set, and a bed made, my father right at the entrance asked my mother to take off his boots, just to set his sovereignty in the marriage.

With fluttering, thick, natural eyelashes, my mother moved in and said demurely, "Please fetch me a glass of water."

The water was right beside her on the table but my father, being a gentleman, rushed to give it to her, first taking his boots off. My mother told me this years later. He did not realize she was establishing a precedent: the law of reciprocity. And later when he learned about it he was implicitly happy he had chosen such a smart wife. My mother's resignation from school right after they married baffled my father. Precisely nine months later, my brother was born.

But the fights had started before. Baba joon had wandering eyes and a gift of gab with women. Years and years later, I asked Baba joon if the popular belief that men were by nature not faithful was true. He freed me from the cultivated distortion. He said, "For every unfaithful man there should be an unfaithful woman." I certainly believed that, but I had wished my mother had heard it, too, in her impressionable years. Or maybe she did not trust women. One thing I was sure of, however, was that she knew my father loved her dearly.

Relying on the Kindness of Strangers: Tears of Tenderness in Jordan

The word Petra launched me to Jordan, of which I knew nothing. This brought about an uproar in some. "Primitive desert Bedouins. Sunni sect hostile to Shia sect from Iran." "A makeshift country with a king from a Saudi clan, drawn by Churchill, to protect British interest. Nothing to see."

All accurate facts. Meeting my Bedouin kin, however, stoked the fire of eagerness in me. Indeed, one of the most lyric pieces of music I've ever heard was a Bedouin folklore that was repeatedly played in buses and taxis.

I met Dave, a retired school principal from Toronto, well studied and with few words, during our flight.

We arrived late in the evening at the Amman airport. After clearing, I detected him in the exit rows of waiting taxis. Dave approached me and wanted to share a ride. "We divide the fare." The cab fare was dirt cheap, but I felt safer having company. He had studied Jordan and knew our destinations were in opposite directions. He said I'd be first to be dropped.

With no Arabic words at his disposal, he negotiated the ride with the man who was overseeing the drivers and a cab arrived. He offered me the back seat, and sat in front with the driver, a real conversationalist with minimal English. The type that gives lots of information during the ride and makes it interesting. As soon as he heard me talk, he said, "You no Canadian! Where from?"

I said, "Iran."

He turned with a fierce face. "Shia?!!" I felt a blow to my safety. He said to David, "Crazy!" Pointing at me. And he produced his iPhone showing a video of a man slashing his back with a curved sword, bleeding profusely, and chanting, "Hossein! Hossein!" The scene was repeated over and over. He continued, "Crazy people. Hossein killed long past. They cry now!"

In his least wordy fashion, Dave said, "I don't know about these people, but where I come from, we do the same!" He turned to me and said, "My folks are Catholics from Ireland."

The driver understood the lack of shock in his response and became silent. He dropped me at my hotel. I did not see Dave again.

I decided never to mention Iran while in Jordan.

The courteous hotel staff helped me with available city maps and attractions. All historical sites were within hours of Amman, and some Roman ruins were within walking distance of the hotel. In the morning, I went for a walk. Amman is built on a hilly desert and, in some areas, houses were built on several closely connected levels. I was walking on a straight street and soon found myself at a level higher, above where I had started, as if I had walked on an invisible curve. After passing a few levels and getting lost and seeing a pile of dirty ice, I found myself at the downtown bus station. I met two American girls from Minnesota, teaching in Amman. Both were competent in Arabic. Both, like me, were dressed in a Western style, though conservatively and I felt very comfortable among the majority of women who were more covered; this was clearly a secular society.

They told me there had been an ice storm a few days before. I had left Toronto on December 27, when the whole city had turned to crystal.

I saw the remnants of the ice storm in the entrance to Petra a few days later, too, in glaring sunshine. The pink city of Petra, carved in the adjacent mountains, was testimony to Arab architectural and artistic prowess, dating back to over 3,000 years BC. And there were far more.

In Umm Qais, over the ruins of a civilization, I met a group of young men, university students who had come to the ruins just to have fun. They were surprised at my ease climbing the ruined walls. This was not a woman's type of activity. They wanted to invite me to a restaurant to celebrate "my New Year." I had forgotten it was New Year's Eve! Their kindness thrilled my heart.

Waiting for the bus to fill before leaving for Amman, the bus owner, a green-eyed, sun-wrinkled Bedouin in traditional robe and headdress, kept offering me coffee and juice.

I have a habit of frequenting churches to light candles and mosques to say prayers when travelling. I arrived in Amman's city centre in the late afternoon. I noticed a mosque. I had an urge, against my better judgment, to enter and say prayers. Sunni Arabs are far more regimented about their prayers compared with a secular Shia from Iran. The gate was open as a mosque is God's house for the needy. But as I was about to enter, I noticed a man looking like a member of the clergy but with no signifying hat, doing something at the fence, looking at me inquisitively. I said, "Salaam" and asked if I could say prayers. He asked in flawless English, "Are you from Iran?" I panicked. He said he was in Iran for three years for comparative religious studies. And, given my look and request to say prayers at that time, he was sure I was from Iran. He kindly guided me to the women's praying area.

The day of my flight back at midnight, I had to see a Roman ruin in the north and a southwest ancient jewel of a town called Madaba in the afternoon. By my calculation, I needed to be back at the hotel at 8 p.m., to get changed, take a taxi at 8:30 p.m., and be at the airport for 9 p.m. A happy-faced teenager with his front teeth missing from sports helped me to transfer to the bus to Mabada. He said his parents, both physicians from Palestine, worked as technicians. Two-thirds of this polite, gentle population of six million were from Palestine, Syria, and other places, fleeing to safety. In the bus to Madaba, men sat beside men, and women beside women, but there was no rigidity about it. I sat in the only available seat, beside a young man. During the hour-long drive, we had a great conversation. He was in his last year of engineering in Amman and was visiting his parents in Madaba on the weekend. I had a feeling that a man looking like the earlier Bedouin bus owner, standing against the front window, kept looking at me. When our eyes finally met, he said something. The young man said the bus owner was asking if I had a hotel reservation in Madaba. I thanked him and said there was no need for a hotel as I was returning with the 6:30 p.m. bus.

But that night there was no 6:30 p.m. bus. We would arrive at 5:45 and the bus would leave at 6 p.m. These hospitable Bedouins were watching me. They knew why I was in Madaba, and that I did not know the bus schedule. Noticing my bewilderment, the young man said, "I'll help you see the map of Jerusalem and bring you back for 6 p.m." We ran to the little sixth-century Greek Orthodox church where there was a detailed mosaic map of Jerusalem on the floor.

On the way back, he showed me a Christmas tree beside a mosque. At the bus depot he asked the driver to wait two minutes, and left. He returned with a bag containing a sandwich, a chocolate bar, an apple, and some mango juice. This youth of twenty-one was the embodiment of the legendary Arab hospitality that had been tattooed in my mind since childhood. My tears flowed and, against the rules, I hugged him gently.

The bus depot was outside my hotel zone and I needed help to get the right taxi. There was a large supermarket close by. I went toward the customer service desk and showed my hotel card. A worker who could speak English was summoned. He was a slight young man with kind green eyes. His English was refined; he just needing practice in conversation.

As we walked outside and he was searching for a cab, he told me he had just graduated from medical school in Syria but, because of the war there, he had to get a job in Jordan to mail his application for U.S. universities. He was holding a Manila envelope for dear life. We exchanged email addresses seconds before he put me in the cab. My tears flowed.

Six months later he emailed me. He was in the U.S. starting his studies. My tears.

They Come in All Shapes and Forms

After nearly three decades, I went to my country of birth and youth and far more: beloved Iran. The visit before this one had been to get married to my Canadian husband-to-be, who'd insisted on coming to Iran to formally ask for my hand.

My parents had been living in Toronto for years and were thrilled to imagine a wedding in a church where they could usher their daughter down a red carpet and deliver her to her future husband. As truly spiritual Moslems, they believed that if the prevailing religion here was Christianity then it would be a church wedding. They had seen in the movies how fathers walk their daughters down the aisle and they loved it. But, of course, my mother wanted to participate, too. This idea was far more exciting than the actual marriage of their daughter, which was of no concern to them.

But Stan wanted to do it the "right way!" That trend dominated our marriage.

The 1975 Iran had burst into modernity and economic prosperity far more than when I left in 1969. The slim layer of intellectual middle class had become stronger. Tehran was as vibrant as New York, luring foreign investors, inviting tourists, soliciting back all brains that had been drained by the U.S. "The army of education» made up of graduates from high school and university were serving two years in the most remote areas cultivating literacy, arts, industry and health care. Everybody danced in the open air at our wedding.

And then a massive political climate change came in 1979, like the rattle of a kaleidoscope, changing the visual field for the onlookers. Not much changed at the core, but women being forced to be covered was an essential feature of this reinvention.

So after nearly three decades since the jubilant wedding, even though I was well versed about being covered and had dressed properly, I felt like Alice walking down the rabbit hole. It was a whole new visual world, but the currency of language had remained the same. Vibrancy had bowed to palpable paranoia. Even the hospitality woven into the Iranian culture now had some degree of deliberation. And yet the beauty at the deepest layer was more not less. The dearth of foreign tourists had been compensated by massive internal tourism. After all, you can spend your whole life travelling in Iran but won't be able to claim you have seen it all.

This estrangement did not change in my subsequent second and third visits, but I was feeling far more adapted after many trips to various parts of Iran.

One was a day trip to an ancient town called Ghazvin, a few hours away from Tehran. A distant relative was my hostess and we opted to get a taxi. A young girl, at the most nineteen years old, was already in the cab. I asked if she lived in Ghazvin and she said no. She had gone to university there but on this particular day she was going to see her boyfriend. She had told her parents that she had an assignment; otherwise, she would not be allowed to go.

I wanted her to give us some tips about Ghazvin. She said we must not use a local taxi in Ghazvin as, in the last three months, multiple dead women had been found on the roads out of the town. Indeed, there was a curfew at sunset. The police department was sure it had been a cab driver, but were puzzled about the motive as the women had not been sexually assaulted nor robbed.

We arrived very early afternoon in the blazing sunshine of June, and said farewell to our young friend.

Soon, we found our way to a major historic mansion with multiple arches and ceramic and wooden artwork, called Aali Ghapu, a replica of a larger one in a more famous city, Esfahan. But this had its own beauty and was adorned with a large, landscaped courtyard with many benches for visitors. We were happy that we were still safe before we walked to the taxi stand.

I searched for a vacant bench in the shade, but detected only one, which already had a lady sitting at one end of it. We approached and asked if we could share the bench and she was most obliging. She said she was waiting for her daughter, who had a piano lesson nearby.

She was reading a local newspaper and, as soon as I glanced over it, I saw that, right at the very top of the front page in bold letters, it said, "The mystery murderer is found!"

Oh, no curfew!

Soon, the three of us were talking about this gruesome event, after she kindly let me read the article. The culprit was a stylish thirty-something housewife, mother of two.

She had been frequenting the affluent cemeteries following a celebration-of-life ceremony where people were dressed up, and wept profusely at the gravesites of the deceased, and at the end, would offer a ride to a middle-aged lady. Offering rides is a common gesture of kindness in Iran, in particular under difficult circumstances, such as coldness, heat, transportation breakdown, or seeing somebody old or stranded. The victim, assuming she was a close friend of the deceased, would accept, and midway through the ride would be asked about her favourite drink, which she'd apparently bought from a store on the way. The content would be mixed with a lethal dose of a tasteless and odorless poison. Soon, the victim would lose consciousness and be robbed of her jewellery, and her body would be thrown on the out-of-town road.

The last victim somehow gets suspicious as she refuses the drink and yet the driver insists and stops to buy one. While she is gone, the passenger leaves the car, registers the plate number, and informs the police. In her rented luxury two-bedroom apartment, police found two school-age children, a drug dealer husband, and a large, locked closet packed with stolen jewellery.

My host and I glanced at each other in a knowing way. They come in all forms and shapes. Imagine the lady next to us could have been *her*, but thank God we were devoid of any jewellery!

Two days later I read in Tehran newspapers that the woman was hanged after a complete investigation and a psychiatric examination. Kudos to their most economic, efficient, and expedited justice system—the same justice system that eliminated scores of political dissenters even before the present regime.

When the psychiatrist asked her why she killed so many women, she answered, "I guess all these years, I have resented my mother, who is a rich woman but refused to help me with my debts."

The psychiatrist then responded, "You are so good at planning a murder, why did you not kill your mother to get all her money as an inheritance, sparing innocent lives?"

She responded, "Listen, you asked me a stupid question. I gave you a stupid answer."

Stories from Rehab: Beyond the Line of Duty!

This place is run like an autonomous, breathing gentle giant. All goes smoothly and I am surrounded by wonderful, courteous, professional staff. Their job definitions are serious and for ten people who go out of their way, there is maybe one who exploits it and skirts the responsibility. Like a housekeeper who will not clean the hall because there are some wheelchairs in his way and it's not in his job definition to move wheelchairs!

My own sleeping giant, however, is coming to life with highly critical eyes. I kept seeing some dried flower petals under my bedside commode and other objects were adding up every morning I opened my critical eyes. Now some of them were two weeks old! I knew I would continue seeing them.

The thought of getting a broom and sweeping the floor grew strong in me—in particular when I spotted a housekeeping person who was the least busy in the lounge. I was sitting there in my wheelchair, my injured leg extended.

I asked him if he worked for the hospital and he said, *yes, in housekeeping.*

I asked if he could give me a little broom so I could clean under my commode. I told him it was great exercise for me.

He said "rooms" were not in his job definition. I explained that I realized that but only wanted a little broom as cleaning that debris seemed not to be in the job definition of the housekeeping staff of the last two weeks.

He looked at me and left.

In a few minutes, he came back with a huge manual sweeper and said that was all he had because he did the halls and garbage cans.

I thanked him a lot and we went to my room. But he insisted on sweeping under the commode and all!

I was very impressed by his kindness. Wow! He really went beyond his line of duty. Now we exchange personal greetings on a daily basis.

LUNCH WITH ROY

I have a lunch date with Roy this Thursday. I am so excited, almost anxious. Could I make it a pleasant, memorable time? I have learned that opportunities happen only once. They keep coming endlessly, but not the same one.

I get a text: "Are you coming?" I was running. I didn't want to be late. I had imagined that I'd be early and 'order a cocktail before Roy arrived.

This was the first time we were having lunch alone for many years. And here I was, late. Three minutes late. Roy had been always punctual and his time very pressured. I didn't need to apologize. I was forgiven.

He was standing outside Sassafraz, a willowy figure so unassuming, looking at my direction with those eyes that melted my heart the first time we met. His eyes have a permanent smile. He was standing outside because he wanted me to choose the table. I knew he did not enjoy having the sun in his face. I chose a safe table on the patio of the walkway. We'd been there before.

I looked at his face and saw the same from years past. And yet we both had changed. Time had sculpted us, bit by bit.

His thin, clean-shaven face, adorned by receding, close-shaved hair, was focussed on the menu. It was Summerlicious time at Sassafraz and the menu featured assorted fancy names. "So, what are you going to eat?" he asked me without taking his eyes from the menu. I knew he wouldn't drink but I still asked, "Any drink?"

"No!" he answered.

I ordered my favourite mojito with Persian candy on the side. Roy indulged me with a sip when I encouraged him to taste it. A man with genuine principles, as always.

He was a small eater. Nothing had changed, even sharing his plate with me. He is a neat eater and I am a sloppy eater. He leaves some food on his plate and I almost have to lick my plate clean. And his, too.

We don't have very much to talk about. But it's a lovely, velvety silence where words are only contamination and noise. I look at his gentle face and my heart melts again.

We used to have lunch every Friday. Roy would come from his work all the way to Cumberland, a location easiest for me. We both loved Sushi Inn, so humble and small, yet with the best service and food. I was always thrilled that Roy wanted to have lunch with me but I was actively praying that he would stop. I had told him my wish and he would just deliver his signature closed-mouth smile.

I would say, "Roy, when are you going to cancel our lunch?" And he would say, "Do you believe in God? When the time comes."

And then one Friday mid-morning he called and said he wouldn't be coming for lunch. No explanation. Roy was reticent. My heart thumped. I asked, "Has it finally happened?" I heard him say "Mmm!" And that was the end of our conversation.

Tears of joy welled in my eyes, though I had lost one of the greatest pleasures in my life.

This lunch was the first since that fateful day. Roy and I were sitting alone, face to face, on Cumberland again. But something was missing. There was the same feeling of incompleteness as in the past.

Nothing had really changed except that both of us had aged a few years.

But our relationship had gotten much deeper and more nuanced. Roy was now a happily married man, a father of two. He had found the love of his life on the very day he cancelled his lunch, a lovely young lady at his work. They were both love, marriage, and family type people. They kindly invited me to their blessed wedding, where my tears of joy flowed.

Roy had to go back to work. He asked the server to bring a take-out box and the bill. I started to finish whatever crumbs and vegetable bits were left on his plate. He said in a soft, admonishing voice, "Do you really need it?" As usual, I only smiled impishly and continued.

We stood up to leave and exchanged a light embrace and soft kisses on the cheek.

He said, "You pick up Colin tomorrow!"

I responded, "I'd love to take Colin and Ian both, if you want."

"No, Mom! You can't handle both." And he rushed to work, leaving me standing on pleasantly busy Cumberland, listening to a lively melody by a Spanish street musician, and savouring our moments together. There may be another time. But, really, I come to life and the future when my grandchildren are around. Without his family, I feel something big is missing, exactly like years ago.

MY MOST PRECIOUS, TRUSTED, AND LOVING MIRROR

A true friend is like a good mirror. It gives you the best reflection of yourself, and yet allows you to see the flaws clearly. It's not about "Mirror, mirror, on the wall, who is the fairest of us all?" It's about "Mirror, mirror, help me be fair to you. So, I can see me fair, too."

It's a difficult combination. This is why true friends are rare commodities. Friendships cannot be forged. They cannot be practised. The combination is a God-given gift. It's such a privilege to be true friends. I have tried a lot to be one to the ones I like, but I could only be one of the two, at any given time: either critical, or blinded by goodness.

So, I feel lucky to have just a few, and to be a true friend to just a few.

It's so heavenly to feel utterly beautiful and at the same time highly alert to one's immeasurable flaws in need of control or management. I think that's the true meaning of unconditional love. A reciprocal process in which one is loath to allow their flaws to hurt the other. Yes, unconditional love certainly does not mean we can stretch ourselves at our beloved's expense. It means how we trust and cherish our beloveds and curtail our hurtful tendencies.

The eternal and relentless desire to be beautiful is to reach that state. How smart are cosmetic companies to help people reach that goal, no matter how superficial it is, and how apparently self-centred the act. The bottom line is that we are searching for that divine state to be good in others' eyes. So, it's not that self-centred. That's why the cosmetics industry is so lucrative and timeless.

I know what a self-centred state is. Every day I feel it to my bones.

Early in the morning with a completely washed face and untidy hair, I look in the mirror and one thought comes to my mind: *God, why did you make me so beautiful? How much time did you spend on ME?*

And in that divine state, I start to demolish my perfection by fussing about cosmetics applied on my face and the management of my hair. The confusing thing is that the more I fuss, the more flawed I feel. And at the end I am humbled to feel one step away from the queen of ugly! I could touch the pain of people who go for cosmetic surgery or other interventions. It's like self-mutilation as there is self-hate in such a pursuit.

How could these paradoxical states exist side by side? So easily. It's about being human. We Tarzan between the two until, hopefully, the pendulum comes to rest close to the middle.

In my vain pursuit of beauty, still active in my sunset days, any new cosmetic item or instruction will be welcome.

A short while ago, I heard from somewhere that lipstick, which is usually applied to the limit nature has designed for lips, could have a much more enhancing effect if applied slightly beyond the natural lip line. I think it was coincident with the cosmetics world pushing for botoxing or using filler for the upper lip.

Wow! What an easy way to add to my beauty. I did apply the lipstick as advised. And as is in my nature, I overdo everything. If a little is good, more is better. I never learn my lesson.

The first wonderful human mirror I faced, a lady with a good sense of beauty, told me. "Oh! What's it about your smile today?" The nice lady had known me for years and was expressing her concern in a polite and sincere way. But the Falstaff in me heard it as: "What a lovely smile you have." A triumphant smile was formed over my brain.

Wow! The enhancement was real. So, in the ensuing hours, as soon as I found myself a mirror, I made another attempt to widen the limit of the lipstick and the more people paid attention to me, the wider the lipstick around my poor lips. What a genius who suggested this simple way to enhance one's beauty!

I was utterly humbled by my newly achieved height in self beautification when I arrived at Oliver & Bonacini at Bayview Village for dinner with my extended family, all coming from a hard day's work.

The first mirror was my truthsayer sister, who looked at me with horror and said, "What have you done? Go to the bathroom fast and clean it!" I thought my cerebral sister had no idea about the little points so necessary in the improvement of our humanity, the simple attempts to be beautiful.

I would ask my daughter, Naseem, as soon as she arrived, so my sister could learn that this new style of applying lipstick, so different from conventional wisdom, was just chic, the fashion of the day.

Naseem had on numerous occasions rescued me from lipstick smeared on my teeth, a dress worn inside out, vegetables caught between my teeth, stains on my clothing, hidden patches of white in my hair, and much more.

My daughter, my best mirror, the one who loved me dearly and was most critical of me, would tell me the truth.

At that moment I detected Naseem approaching hastily and, without my prompting, in a most concerned way, addressing me, she said, "Mom! Why have you made yourself like a clown? Your lipstick!"

That blissful unconditional love of this young woman, my daughter, my true friend, made me rush to the elegant Bayview Village ladies' room as if running for my dear life. Running to regain my dignity. The poor mirror was showing the clown and I was seeing it.

A good washing allowed all of us to eat in peace and genuine happiness. I did not feel I had to be beautiful. Neither did I have to be a clown in pursuit of attention. Falstaff was gone. Thank you,

Shakespeare, for your universal truth. Love was all over. And I was deeply thankful to have a sister like Vida.

EGGPLANTS AND MY COMPETITIVE NATURE

Keeping some level of decent physical activity during the Covid-19 quarantine, after a few weeks, became somewhat challenging. It felt like being a passenger on a bus or train that had come to an unpredictable and abrupt stop. The first thing was to regain my balance. And then appraise the situation and wait until the bus started moving. But bus remained still. And was not going to move. And somehow passengers had dispersed and I was alone.

Another attempt to regain a new balance. Limbs had to move. I had to remove myself from my virtual constrained space into a much larger real space—a much larger cage of my own house bordered by quarantine.

To resume some measure of activity, I still needed to adjust myself within the perceived cage. It was large enough. I could really move. It was far from the situation that Gregor Samsa found himself trapped in. But if I did not move, my fate would be similar to the protagonist of Kafka's masterpiece, *Metamorphosis*. Although with no butterfly to follow. It would be complete banishment from the realm of being. And I was not ready for that.

Expanding my mobility, however, was fraught with danger. Corona was known to have special interest in elderly people. The quarantine started in mid-March 2020 and by mid-May Canada had lost over

213

6,000 people, over 80 percent from nursing homes. The majority of lost lives were from Toronto and Montreal.

Hamlet's dilemma, to be or not to be, was transfigured as "To venture out, expand my mobility beyond the confine of my house, or stay confined?"

I want to die young. I have no fear of death. It's life I love; I want to keep it as long as I have my total health and experience love.

I can't afford Hamlet's dilemma. I will follow the expression, "He who hesitates is lost." Better in its original form: "The woman that deliberates is lost," from Cato.

I shall venture outside the confines of my house. Armed with my mask I soldiered out one early morning.

The usual walk way felt strange. I had not stepped out for a few weeks. The street looked deserted. The very few passersby made sure to distance themselves in a deliberate way. An act of courtesy. The birds were serenading the bright, pleasant, warm, sunny day. The spring had sprouted out like Vivaldi's depiction of it. Trees so voluptuous with bold green that was the opposite of my cowardly state. Some lucky houses had their front lawns ornamented with freshly opened tulips, daffodils, and fragrant Narcissus. Not mine, with a minimal share of celestial energizer.

The walk up Banbury Road felt surreal. Once I arrived at York Mills Road, a sign of the continuation of life, cars on the road, became more evident. Traffic was very light, though cars drove faster than usual, as if the drivers were also feeling surreal.

More people appeared. Most did not have masks on, but were observant of the need to distance. At the corner of Leslie and York Mills, the sign of our local grocery store, Longo's, became visible. And soon I noticed a line of around ten people standing about two metres apart, stretching out from the entrance.

I remembered that the quarantine law dictated that only a limited number of people could be in the store at any given time. Standing in line is an intolerable experience for me. But I had an overwhelming urge to join this one, even though I did not need any groceries. The urge was strong.

The feeling was related to a competitive streak in me. It had alarmed me when I was just about fourteen, but had also propelled me from early on. And it was going to brutally dictate my journey in life.

During summers in my birthplace, Iran, our family would go for two or three months to cool, rural areas, where we enjoyed scenes of farms, vineyards, fruit orchards, cattle, sheep, and goats. Shepherd boys, farmers, and beautiful, pristine nature were common sights etched in my memory. Every day, there was some form of activities.

Climbing up the nearby rocky mountain with little greenery very early in the morning was a must. Always accompanied by Mom. But the very first time I was entrusted to lead on my own was in the summer of my fourteenth birthday. My four younger siblings were my charges, the youngest only four years old. They had no choice but to follow me, the two youngest ones holding my hands.

I had every intention of reaching the little usual peak. But just before we reached it, I noticed a new peak that I had not noticed when I had been a blind follower. *We had to reach it.* The same view appeared before we reached the second peak, and then more. *I had to reach the summit.* None of these were the summit. Only steps to summit. My trusting little sibs were stoically following, hoping the treat time would come as soon as I decided. Their quiet patience brought me to my senses. How long could I chase this illusion of summit? Soon, the dark may come and its attendant dangers. I felt really alarmed. I declared the treat time and accepted my defeat, and soon descended.

Now entering the grocery store by standing in line felt like approaching the summit. I took my place in the line. In fewer than fifteen minutes, I entered the store. It felt like an amusement park. I went up and down the aisles of usual staples just because I could. I felt so light and free. I had to buy something because I could. I picked up two eggplants, one of the most versatile ingredients, which could be used to create many different and delicious dishes. I paid for them and left the store shortly after. When I exited, I saw that the line now stretched much longer than it was before I arrived. The sense of victory in me was immense.

The experience was very close to participating in a regional test for entering medical school. It was one of the peaks I had to reach before arriving at the final summit.

In my mind's eye, I was able to see that what I got from medical school was the equivalent of the delicious eggplants: some basic information that had to be used in understanding the complexities of life. Allowing me to continue climbing from peak to peak. And finally declaring defeat, with great relief, that the real summit was the recognition of my unlimited limitation.

ARMENIA THE LAND OF HAY . . . HAYASTAN

When lost in the streets of Armenia, or at a loss as to how to communicate during a purchase in a store, Hayastanis look through you, not at you, and a wordless dialogue ensues: *Why are you making strangers of us? We've known each other from atom.*

A Hayastani engages and overcomes you to accept the fact that you are not lost; you are at home. Like home is where you are. Don't make strangers with your home, buddy. And that's despite the language barrier. It's too insignificant.

It's unclear when Hayastan was renamed Armenia. But it is still the name of the country in its spoken language. On top of one of the highest hills in the capital, Yerevan, the statue of Mother Hayastan greets the entire city.

I went to Armenia mainly because my high school buddy, whose ancestors were from there, had enticed me with her passionate talk about the ordeal Armenians had gone through in the last few centuries. Seda is a woman of steely resolve concealed by a silky hijab of compassion and kindness. She is not a do-gooder. She approaches a worthy cause and researches it multidimensionally, negotiates like a Berber until she achieves mutual agreement. And then she puts her time and soul into it. She cared a lot during the aftermath of the 1988 earthquake, which left 25,000 to 50,000 people dead and far more injured, and sank the economy to the level of national poverty.

She listened nostalgically when her family and friends brought stories from their homeland. But she was just waiting to be nudged by her wild travelling friend.

She speaks Armenian fluently. I trusted her formidable intelligence and common sense and gave her my blind trust for our trip.

Shortly before our trip, a historical event was happening in Armenia: the election of a long-time activist/journalist to power. The existing regime was not going away easily. Some political upheaval was in the air. But Nikol Pashinyan, perceived as a saviour, was elected. The Velvet Revolution won over long and hard corruption. Previously, they had won a Rose Revolution. Every Hay had protested by getting dressed and entering their parliament holding a rose in their hand.

The beautiful, green, fertile hilly and mountainous earth, a shrunken little land left from its glorious world-conquering days, boasting its ancient cathedrals, churches, and its original alphabet, is inhabited by people who have survived many ordeals. They wear the footprint and dust of a long imperial history, a genocide, a century of brutal communism, a devastating earthquake, and economic wreckage in its wake. But there was the scent of sweet hope and happy Armenian music everywhere in the air.

In Yerevan, we stayed in a house recommended by a friend to Seda. It was steps away from a heritage house converted to a restaurant belonging to the heart-stealing singer Charles Aznavor. His parents had to leave, like most Armenians during those impossibly hard times, and he had found fame and fortune in France, and shared it generously with his people. We ate a nice lunch there.

In our first morning, I was able to get cautious Seda's agreement to walk along a major street near our residence, but the walk ended with our finding ourselves on the top of a hill where Charles Aznavor's elegant museum was located, looking down at Yerevan, and up at

Mount Ararat, with no path to descend but cascading stairs. Thousands of them, it seemed.

Each level ended in a garden and an adorned fountain. The late August mid-morning was broiling us with brilliant sun in a cloudless sky. It looked like eternity, a thousand stairs?! Only later did we learn that the escalators were just next to us. By the time we reached the garden court level of Cascade Square, Seda had gone through dehydration and an electrolyte imbalance, and was shaken from head to toe. And I was in silent agony and remorse.

We dumped ourselves on the chairs of the first restaurant and Seda breathlessly said to the server, "Please bring me a bucket of water!" And she never trusted me with a short walk again.

Cascade Square was surrounded by clusters of burgeoning cafés and restaurants, with local and foreign cuisine, offering the most delicious bread, lavash, and creative, tasty dishes exclusive to Armenia. This structure, like Genocide Tower, is a monument celebrating a resilient people, a phoenix rising from its ashes. Evening dances on Fridays with lively folk music bring all Yerevan, young and old, to Cascade Square, where they dance in unison, declaring their unity.

Seda had arranged a local driver to take us around, short and long distances. His name was Ashod, and he was respectfully addressed as Baron Ashod. He was a true gentleman, not a rare commodity in Armenia. In reality, he was an unpaid tour guide. Twice, he drove us to the edge of Mount Ararat, now a property of Turkey, but the road did not allow progress.

We met a few of Seda's lovely friends and one, a physician, left both of us with an immense sense of gratitude. Besides imparting objective views and facts, Dr. Ruzanna Stepanyan offered us a kindness that shall remain unrequited. This, despite her heavy professional responsibilities.

Ruzanna took us to the heart and soul of Armenia. Serial weddings and baptisms in an ancient church, an artist creating from multimedia who had built his own charming house in a small land filled with fruit trees—all ripe when we visited, and ready to be dried soon, a major

Armenian delicacy. I purchased a little sculpture of Noah's Ark, which was supposed to have landed on top of Mount Ararat.

Ruzanna took us to a traditional restaurant made of numerous gazebo-like dining rooms with handmade wooden furniture, located in a huge acreage in the form of an amusement park, with gardens, fountains, playgrounds, and adorned pathways.

A concealed indoor kitchen from which the skilled servers emerged with carts, carrying the ordered food, crowned the complex.

Beside this complex there was a trout pond irrigated by fresh water.

The bill for a delicious lunch was, as usual, shamefully low and an expectation for a tip was zero.

We had a tour inside the bakery of this complex, where the Armenian-grown wheat turned to flour, passed through various stages until it was smacked to the wall of a smouldering deep pit by the skillful hands of professional baker women. Within a few minutes inside the fire, a delicious lavash was produced.

Noticing our fascination with their work, the workers gifted us one lavash.

What generosity!

Our overnight trips to Georgia and Artsakh deserve their own stories. But vodka made from grape juice locally called Oghi, Aragh, was equally good in these countries blessed by an abundance of grape wines.

Shortly after the end of our trip, the Armenian prince of melodic songs, after a long life of making people's hearts sing, passed away.

Shame recedes when conscience arrives: From finger painting on to a work in progress

Once I read a personal story by an accomplished writer, recalling when she found herself screaming violently on a stretcher, being rushed toward the delivery room. Her painful wails subdued the din of the busy hospital, and exhausted the supportive nursing staff, who failed to reassure her that her pain was not dangerous and soon would disappear. This was her second normal delivery.

She had no fear of the pain, which was heralding the arrival of her second baby. She wrote that she was petrified at that moment as her second book was being published, and the thought of how it would be received filled her with fear for the court of public opinion and the ensuing humiliation.

There, her life would be scrutinized and every weakness and personal blemish would be exposed. The occasion of delivery gave her chance to express her perception of being tortured, condemned by her human shame. She went on to win many awards.

Every word written on a page is accompanied by that inner shame. Even though humanity is a euphemism for being flawed, the illusion of being flawless is like an eternally seductive banner held over the mind's eye, interfering with consciousness. Shame is our essence in isolation. It makes a labyrinth that even a hero like Theseus and the love and wisdom of Ariadne cannot navigate.

King Minos, the ruler of Crete, was revenged upon by angry Zeus, and was humiliated by the birth of his defective offspring, with the body of a human and the head of a bull. He commissioned the legendary architect Daedalus to make a structure so complicated that nobody could get access to the Minotaur, and that prevented him from leaving the compound.

In Greek mythology, the Minotaur, the bull-headed man, is an allegory, the visual representation of shame. But unlike the mythical Minotaur, who was slain by Theseus through the guidance of wise and loving Ariadne, our shame cannot be eliminated as it contains our primary resources such as energy, talent, artistic disposition, curiosity, judgment and self-observation.

Once self-observation is blocked, the task gets assigned to others, it's farmed out to the external world. We worry about what others think of us rather than being our own judge. This keeps us in hiding. Our own conscience does not develop as the root of the conscience, the inner judge, is in absorbed love. "I could be good enough, loved, rather than perfect."

In the Minotaur's case it is the love of his sister, Ariadne, for Theseus that brokers the discovery. She gives Theseus a ball of wool to unravel as he enters the labyrinth while she holds one end. He can't get lost.

For ordinary mortals like us, our ability to absorb love allows us to look at ourselves, face the flaws, accept them, and manage them. We cannot, nor do we need to, eradicate them. Our flaws are forever the source of primary energy, which can be used as fuel in our journey toward self-improvement, a perpetual state of a work in progress.

Self-exposure through social contact, artistic expression, creativity, producing a worked-up state such as cooking from raw ingredients, and writing offers various paths we can use to navigate our labyrinth of shame. When our conscience arrives, shame disappears.

I enjoy writing and sometimes it's bigger than me, forcing me to let it out. And every word resonates with my shame.

The other day, my daughter Naseem, a published author, complimented me for the first time on my most recent story.

My God! Receiving a compliment from a published author?! I became giddy.

I asked her if she considered me like a child using crayons. The status was too high for me, but I was going to humbly accept it.

The Lady with the Pen responded: More like finger painting.

I gratefully accepted the accolade.

I am welcoming my shame right at the entrance of my psychological labyrinth exposed to the public, with gallons of paint and hopefully some ink.

NOSTALGIA! DON'T LOOK BACK

The Greek word nostalgia, indicating the pain of yearning for home, has evolved into yearning for the past. Odysseus after pursuing war for years, kept wishing to be back home. He was nostalgic for what he remembered from the past. King Solomon advised against looking at the past. He had the magic ring that easily transported him to past and future. He knew better that nostalgia, searching for the past, was a total waste of time. And I am sure wise and most brutal King Solomon was equally against searching for the future. But I keep falling into nostalgia, and cherishing it until I face the beauty of present.

The other day I was kindly invited to see a rehearsal of The Nutcracker ballet at the Four Seasons Centre for the Performing Arts, by my daughter-in-law Julia. Tchaikovsky not having married nor having children, certainly preserved his youthful spirit. This is well demonstrated in many passages in this Christmas visual and auditory delight. Nutcracker for me is a Christmas must and I received the invitation with joy. Julia is a ballet buff and is encouraging the love of ballet in her daughter Iris. My three-year-old granddaughter certainly was an exemplary audience member and watched the whole suite with rapt attention.

Now that there are far more colourful vistas in my rear-view mirror, every present experience activates a cascade of corresponding memories of the sweet past ecstasies of being young, in love, and motherhood. In my joyful dance and bath in the rainbow of mothering three wonderful children, at times I was stricken by the thunder and lightning of fate, but none had the power to reduce the intensity of that pleasure. Quite contrarily, the blows gave me the resilience to bounce back and use any adverse event as a launching pad. Move on and see more vistas, more options.

So, going to see The Nutcracker with my son's family brought the deluge of memories of rituals to attend any child-worthy shows when our children were very young. And far more. We were living in Guelph then, and driving less than 100 kilometres on weekends in any weather, was no deterrent.

The O'Keefe Centre, today named the Meridian Hall, was the ultimate place to go for every top-notch performance, opera, ballet, orchestral suite, musical and dramatic play. With its soft red cushioned chairs, the modestly ornate theatre had a simple elegance. The grand cultural atmosphere commanded formal dress, perfume, and the utmost courtesy from the audience. The subscriptions made neighbours of patrons who felt obliged to acknowledge each other. Children were only expected for child-oriented performances. Not for a second did I entertain any doubt in my mind that our very young children could be anything but the most desirable patrons.

Across the street from O'Keefe Centre on Front Street were a few restaurants attracting hungry post- and pre-performance patrons for lunch or dinner.

Our post-matinee lunches were frequently at Penelope or Shopsy's Deli. Two different genres, but both child-friendly. Penelope, which eventually moved from its original location and is now completely shuttered, served authentic Greek cuisine. Shopsy's, right at the corner of Yonge and Front, was somehow more entertaining. The crowds were so large that they would not take reservations. We had to go in and be hopeful that we would be called soon to a table. While waiting, generous trays of some form of grilled deli foods with a gourmet mustard container would be offered around by a server with a great smile. I always thought I ate far more from the sampling tray than my actual ordered food. The vibrant environment and hustle and bustle of staff trying to please made us go there frequently.

The afternoon I was invited to see The Nutcracker, I was a bit early and so took a walk through the highly ornamented elegant lobby of the adjacent Four Season's Hotel. As I was ambling along, I noticed a sign for Shopsy's Deli, a place far away in my rear-view window but filled with glitter and joyful sounds. I was flooded by images of our family highly dressed up ushering three under-five-year-old children dressed for Sunday, walking along the aisles of the O'Keefe Centre after a lovely performance, beaming with immense gratitude, and discussing going to Shopsy's. The glitter would follow us until we were seated in a lively, no-rush environment for a hearty meal.

I had not even seen Shopsy's for a few decades since those days.

I thought to myself how lovely it would be if Neil and Julia agreed to have dinner there and I could meet the glorious past in the present.

As soon as I met Neil at the ballet I told him about Shopsy's being so close. Neil's eyes. Oh my God! Neil's eyes! Those talking eyes, which give you a book in a few seconds, were not mirroring my imagined fun. And he reaffirmed my visual perception by saying, "Mom! Shopsy's is not the same as you remember!"

I said, "Oh, that bad? We should not go?" He responded, "We'll go but it won't be the same."

We went and it was not the same. All glitter, hustle and bustle, extreme attention to pleasing, the large, juicy corned beef and the other delicatessen specialties were missing. The whole thing was missing. Most importantly, I was missing! It was a cold bar-like restaurant, lodged in a lively Irish pub! It was as if my memory was totally false. The food? I'd never go back.

And then I noticed my granddaughter moving around in her seat, drawing, painting on a wet napkin on the table, asking questions of her doting parents about the immediate present. She was feeling at home in Shopsy's. I was transported to the present. Indeed, it was so delightful that I could not waste it by going back. Iris was all the tinsel and glitter with a large front window into the future. No room for nostalgia. Thank you, King Solomon.

I wonder—if poor Marcel Proust had been able to connect to the present, could he have written his seminal work *In Search of Lost Time*? All seven volumes of it?

Thank you, Iris.

Relying on the Kindness of Strangers: Immeasurable Generosity

It was my third trip to Iran after nearly forty years. The occasion was the fortieth anniversary of my graduation from medical school. It was as poignant as delightful to see those eighteen-year-olds who were sitting on the bench with me pursuing similar goals for the next seven years and then having no more contact. It was as if nobody had changed. Just greyed. The same kind, gentle faces who were always courteous when we started as total strangers.

After this memorable night, my host, Azar, and I travelled to places I had not visited before, each place so unique that it felt like visiting different countries. Since the politically induced eclipse of tourism in Iran from 1979 to the present, the bulk of tourists there are Iranians, enjoying the vast cultural diversity and varied terrains, sometimes travelling only 200 kilometres from their homes.

Hamadan the capital of ancient Persia was one of the cities we visited. Beside its own charm, Hamadan is home to Avicenna (Abu Ali Sina), a late tenth-century, early eleventh-century thinker with expertise in many areas like all polymaths of ancient times. He is known to be the father of modern medicine. His mausoleum is a work of modern architecture. Sina lived like a refugee in his own time due to political upheavals. Hamedan was his chosen home.

The tomb of Esther, the Hebrew queen of Persia, married to King Xerxes (Khashayar Shah) alongside with her cousin and guardian Mordecai, has been preserved in the centre of the city for over 2,500 years.

A bit away from Hamadan, we visited Ghar e Ali Sadr (Cave of Ali Sadr), the largest water cave in the world, going all through the rocky mountain that covers it. The transparent, shimmering water in the lighted cave gives it a mysterious quality. We met scores of schoolchildren visiting, like at most historical sites and natural icons in Iran.

After a round trip we were back in Tehran two days before my flight back home. Early the next morning I left to do the last banking and the only shopping.

Breathing in Tehran is a serious health hazard due to the poorly refined oil used for transportation and heavy traffic. But early in the morning it feels fresh and crisp, as if some magic hand had vacuumed all the gasoline from the air overnight.

To beat the intractable traffic jam there are many means of transportation. One of the fastest is a low-fare cab that drives on a straight line. These taxis are registered and practically cover all of the central area.

Most people take the cab for a short distance rather than walking.

My friend's house is far from downtown but on a straight path, and as soon as I arrived on the street, still very clear, a cab stopped for me. There were a few passengers along the way for a short distance.

In the bank I withdrew all my American dollars—in the neighbourhood of $U.S.1,000—and left my friend's address and telephone number as reference. Then I went to do my shopping with the rest of Persian money, at a boutique that sold certified authentic fine arts. I chose three necklaces with replicas of the insignia of the Xerxes dynasty. The gifts had to be very light so they could be carried in my little handbag, which contained my phone, camera, hairbrush, toothbrush, some cosmetics, my passport, airplane ticket, and all my cards and cash.

I was so happy to be done, and had started to have the last look at the Tehran streets around me, and the ever-present Alborz Mountain at the far end north of the city, when I noticed a dairy store.

The memory of Persian crème fraiche (khameh), a silky, thick cream as light as air took control of my legs. In the little store, which was well stocked with fresh dairy products, I bought crème fraiche, yogurt, and cheese. I was so excited that I had not left Iran without having khameh. This would be our lunch, wolfed down with freshly baked bread.

Now I had a rather heavy shopping bag in my hand as well as my handbag, but I managed to hail a cab. There were two passengers already in the cab and a few more came with the departure of the old ones.

By the time I arrived at my destination, I was sitting between two passengers, and there was one in front beside the driver. I had prepared my fare in advance and paid and left. The traffic was dense but fast. I shifted my load and suddenly I noticed I had left my handbag in the cab. It was zooming right past before my eyes and the driver was totally unaware of my desperate hand waves and yelling.

I could not register the licence plate number. It was just a white cab. I walked to my friend's home, sad, panicky, and stunned. I told Azar what had happened. She immediately got the relevant telephone numbers: the police, the central cab company, its lost and found centre. They all said the same thing: without the licence plate number, there was no chance to identify the car. If the driver found it he would return it. But the passengers, there would be too many, like one new passenger every five minutes or less.

It was Saturday, the beginning of the week in Iran, and the weekend for the Canadian consulate.

My dream of enjoying a light lunch of crème fraîche disappeared with my appetite. There was nothing to be done until Monday when the consulate opened.

We were sitting stiffly in silence, and shame was added to my misery, for having put my host in such a difficult situation.

It was after 8 p.m. when Azar's phone rang. I heard her saying: "Yes, she is here!" And then she offered me her phone. It was the driver! He said he'd found my handbag open with money bursting out of it in the backseat when he arrived home. And he'd gone through its content and found a bank receipt that had my name and telephone number on it. He would have brought it to me but he lived far away and no longer had gas in his car. He gave me his address.

Azar called a taxi from the agency, a safe and expensive mode of transportation. We had to wait half an hour, and travel for an hour to arrive in a southern suburb of Tehran with very humble row rental houses.

I saw the driver's face for the first time. A young man looking too tired. He welcomed us to his rooming house, which was furnished with a fake, machine-made Persian carpet, in the middle of which there was a tiny oil stove over which a Persian dish (Abgousht) was being cooked, emitting a very delicious familiar aroma. There were no other items in the small room but my handbag, laying on the carpet half open, money gushing out of it. They had delayed eating their dinner, feeling obliged to share it with us. His young wife, holding their baby girl, was looking at us kindly, genuinely sharing my happiness.

We sat down on the floor and thanked them for offering their dinner and excused ourselves for having to rush back.

Then to the business. He was adamant about receiving no reward. It was his responsibility to return my property and he would be paid by the happiness it had brought for him.

I told him that I needed to be happy too by sharing with him through a reward. And therefore, I would mention a figure and if he did not smile, I would mention a bigger figure until he smiled.

I started: $U.S.300. Persian money was, and increasingly is, badly undervalued.

Suddenly, he opened his mouth, not quite like Cheshire Cat as there was enormous joy in his eyes, and said, "I cannot accept it."

For greedy me, I felt relief at his immeasurable generosity accepting $300, however up to this very moment, until my end on earth, I believe all the money belonged to him.

I am still in disbelief, thinking of the number of passengers stepping in and out of the cab over the ten hours after I left, and not one touching the bag. Human goodness has no bound.

I did eat my crème fraîche the next morning before I left for the airport.

My fine art necklaces, Forouhar, Xerxes's heritage were not liked by the recipients.

RELYING ON THE
KINDNESS OF
STRANGERS: KINDNESS
IN MALAYSIA

When in Singapore, the city state is so small and is basically a strategic hub devoid of any charm, notwithstanding its modern, wonderous monuments and buildings. Charm rules in old neighbourhoods with its nearby ancient attractions. Its legendary cleanliness gets only a passing mark. It's cleaner than Paris and London and New York. And not far from Toronto.

Malaysia was just next door, provider of cheap service manpower for Singapore. Rich in Buddhist temples and ancient mosques. I decided to see it.

One attractive old mosque, Sultan Abu Bakr, was in a small town called Johor. It is south of Kuala Lumpur, bordering on Singapore, with mountainous forests and attractive beaches. One brief estimate from a local map indicated that it was, at most, a half an hour's pleasant walk from the bus station.

I asked people around me, pointing to the photo of the mosque, which way I should start. All, without saying a word, made an "impossible" facial expression and kindly waved their hands toward a bus.

They smiled when I moved my hand to the left or right as to what was the correct direction.

So, I started to walk in a direction that seemed going toward the mosque, which now from the reality of the street looked to be on an elevated part of the city. There was a chorus of "No! No! Bus!" as I thanked them and continued.

This people did not know my love for walking and underestimated the tourists' capacity for enjoying simple things.

The November sun in the late morning was generously sending its golden rays from a cloudless blue sky. I kept looking at the mosque and took my direction from estimating visually if I was getting closer to it. And I was getting closer because the mosque was becoming larger. But the longer I walked in the city streets, and I was now perspiring, the more crevices appeared on the path. One was on a straight highway with minimal shoulder to walk on. That by itself was at least half an hour.

I knew I was not getting lost but the flat distance on the map did not show all the ups and downs and elevation on the road. I had finished the highway part and was again on the city premises when I noticed the roar of a motorcycle and then it stopping in front of me.

A young man with a moustache and a face replete with rivulets of sweat, turned to me with a smile, and asked me to let him take me to the mosque. Whatever he missed in the English language was swept away by his sincerity and kindness. He said he'd saw me in the bus station and when he realized I was not taking the bus, he'd decided to go home and get his motorcycle and find me!!! He said it was a long way and it was too hot for me.

I was nearly crying, being showered by this cascade of tenderness. But a rapid calculation took place in my mind. The mosque was winking at me; I was almost touching it, but this time I knew better.

It wouldn't be minutes. Just another half an hour. And also, I was terrified by motorcycles.

And, too, getting a ride with a stranger in a strange country, even in a Tesla, was not for me.

I thanked him sincerely and convinced him that I was really enjoying my walk. He kindly did not insist and left.

By that time, it was early afternoon, at least three hours on foot. I was not even near fatigue, never mind exhaustion.

After a few more streets, I reached the foot of a hill where, suddenly, the mosque disappeared. Soldier on. It was beautiful sunshine not rain. The sight of a hill always brings me exhaustion.

Almost an hour later on top of the hill, I saw the mosque perching at some distance. A few more blocks and there I was at its open gate. I started to climb the stairs, hearing prayers out loud, when a soft voice informed me that it was not open to women at this hour. I have no visual memory of seeing the mosque as I was standing beside it. Just the image I kept walking toward. I respected the rule with a bit of regret.

There was no place to rest, I just walked toward the back of the mosque and from the top I saw the bus station right underneath on the street below. Downhill makes me happy. In a few minutes, I was at a coconut stand, where the local vendor with a traditional hat was piercing hole in the coconuts, in demand for a dollar. Suddenly, I became aware of my dehydration and an unbearable thirst. The young vendor looked at me with such care, being far more aware of my condition than I was. He let me drink the milk and then scraped all the soft part inside and offered the shell to me. The taste was a combination of ZamZam water and manna from heaven.

Within a few minutes I was on the bus, just a half an hour's ride to the station.

Now Indonesia was calling.

"Give Me Something . . . Give Me Anything." And My Cup Runneth Over

South Africa was fascinating in a multidimensional way. Geographically rich with a multitude of fertile landscapes, and terrains loaded with diamond and gold and more. Demographically, the mosaic of an overwhelmingly Black majority and an underwhelmingly white minority, is in an enduring reconciliation process in the wake of a heroic, determined revolt against the segregation of the decades.

And historically, because of its fall and rise through time immemorial.

The Dutch settlers gave their invasion and brutal abuse of the invaded host country religious meaning. Their reading of the holy book guided them toward a promised land, which was waiting for them to reach unbounded prosperity. The holy book was accurate about the real estate value of the promised land, but I am not sure if it sanctioned using its residents as slaves and free labour.

Hardship, however, has a positive side in human life. Only under its extreme ruling our DNA will mutate to bring the kind of Nelson Mandela, Martin Luther King, Jr., and Mahatma Gandhi. The resilience of such a fortitude is palpable in Africa. And it can be seen here and there outside of tourist traps.

As we were travelling from city to city and village to village, mostly highlighted by geographic and ecologic marvels, other less emphasized gems were sprinkled on our way. I picked a large avocado that touched my head when I was walking under a huge tree with leafy branches beaded by avocados in the courtyard of one of our hotels. I bought bags of fresh macadamia nuts on dirt roads, a pound for a dollar.

We saw the most fashionably dressed young women with locally designed costumes that were utterly modern. They kindly allowed me to take photos of them, being in a rush to go back to their desk at work. The radiance of colour and it's made-to-wear-for-real-life design was far away from the impractical outfits one sees on catwalks of haute couturiers.

The outdoor sculptures blended with majestic nature were poetic. The circular golden tiny hills visible from highways running along Johannesburg were cyanide-infiltrated soil around gold mines, so beautiful they make anybody think of gold. Our tour guide recalled how, as a child he used to play on those hills, as nobody knew the purification of gold needs help from this lethal substance.

In one village, a tourist destination we saw a colony of penguins twice the size of doves resting or meandering among the boulders off the coast of the Atlantic Ocean. We were walking along a wide dirt path that had been flattened and smoothed by human feet, with random large trees on both sides. The blue of the sky and ocean were joined. We had arrived at the end of our morning expedition and were approaching our lunchtime, enjoying a tranquil walk to a local restaurant.

The sun rays travelling through the branches were caressing and pleasantly warm. I heard a rhythmic soft music. A few metres ahead under the canopy of a large tree, there were about ten or more children with sparkling black skin who were playing rhythmic music with the most unfathomable instruments, singing softly, and dancing. As I got closer, the age of children, boys and girls, well nourished, clean and colourfully dressed, and engaged in a serious manner in their performance, seemed to be below ten. The girls had their hair nicely styled in braids and decorated, and were accessorized by multiple ornamental beads, anklets, bracelets and rings. Some were producing a rhythmic melodic sound by hitting a stick on a wooden or metal object or a rock. Some danced in synchronicity and harmony, indicating a disciplined choreography, and all sang. They paid little attention to the passersby and nobody seemed to stay and watch them. Later, I was told by my group that they deliberately ignored them as it was a staged begging!

As the dance stopped, I watched their little brilliant ebony faces and the diamonds of their eyes and the clear dignity in their expression. They looked busy preparing for the next act. I noticed a battered little plastic pail on the ground.

To me they were classical street musicians and dancers, no different than the ones who play in the streets of Toronto when the cold stops being biting.

Their music was enchanting from the heart of Africa and their dance was disciplined and practiced. And there was absolutely no soliciting.

I always carry some useful objects in my little purse for such occasions—mostly plenty of pens, little bars of soap, and little shampoo bottles. I started to give them to the children, and I was counting— I finished at number ten. But there was this beautiful little doll barely seven years old who was standing beside me like a baby goddess of patience and staring at my hand moving in and out of my purse.

I said, "Oh, I have finished and there are eleven of you. Her brilliant eyes were fastened to my purse, patiently and silently enduring the delayed justice. I rummaged through my purse again while saying, "I don't have anything else. Let me see if I can find something," while I thought: maybe I'll give her money, aside from the money I put in the communal pail.

At that moment, she raised her glittering diamonds upward and said, "Give me something . . . give me anything," in perfect English.

It was as if she had read my mind. She wanted a souvenir, not money. She was in rush, as the group had started a new session, and I was in rush, too, as I was left behind on this rural road and could become easily lost, a notorious specialty of mine.

My hand touched my travel-sized, heart-shaped, pink-framed mirror. I took it out and showed it to her. The satisfaction in the deep night of her eyes was beyond words. And the memory she left in my mind by the generosity of her spirit keeps warming my heart. "My cup runneth over" is the closest I have to express my gratitude for her gift.

"Grandma, See my Band-Aid? There is No Cut. Nobody Has Hurt Me!"

My little grandson Colin not quite four and perfectly healthy, has a habit of wanting to wear a Band-Aid. Sometimes it's on one of his tiny fingers, sometimes on his arm, and sometimes on his leg. It seems to me he just wakes up in the morning and decides he needs to express a harmless pain in his delicate existence.

When Band-Aids were originally introduced to Colin because of a cut or scratch, if I happened to see him, I would say, "Oh my God! What happened? How were you hurt? Let Grandma kiss your booboo, and take the pain away and make it heal." He was so delighted to become familiar with the magic of love.

Nowadays, those Band-Aids may be applied for no reason. Yet my encounter meets him with the same concern and emotional drama. And this is why, when he presents the Band-Aided part, he always verifies immediately that nobody has caused his booboo. See! There is no cut! Grandma's kiss still works like magic.

Colin's transparency is so beautiful. Children always make the icicles gathered around my heart melt and form puddles in my eyes, and will turn to a balm on my unexplainable inner invisible timeless booboos. How difficult it is for children to relate their pain, discomfort, and hurt to others. How could they be understood? For me it's not easy to relate and have clear communication with an adult with a developed tongue. But with children, I miss a lot. Far more than with adults.

I can relate to their pure joy, but not to their pain. In this regard, I see childhood to be too long. Agonizingly long.

How could a baby express the pain of just bursting into this world? The birth cries give utter pleasure to concerned adult ears. Oh! The baby is alive and well.

Maybe I am reliving my own adaptation to the world. This unknown pain in babies, like my grandson's booboos, is what is called, in adulterated jargon, technical language, "narcissistic pain." There is no cause for it except having to adapt to the external world. To life. But we adult humans have to put logic, sequence, and reason to the pain, and finally to blame it on some cause. And are we not surrounded by many legitimate ones?

Starting with the adults who were lost themselves, yet helplessly tried to look after us. Most of us come away from childhood intact, sometimes from gruesome circumstances. But the booboo of being alive is always present.

If only we could see the pain that way, it could respond to a self-applied Band-Aid, the way Colin does it, and life would be a much more hospitable habitat. It could be celebrated rather than wasted on grief for having unexplainable pain, which we like to ascribe to something tangible. And so, often, we find the apparent cause and dig it deeper and deeper and it keeps making sense—but we miss the fact that it does not take the pain away. Then what's the reason for digging it deeper?

The amount of precious time and energy wasted in simple "understanding," to me, is worse than polluting the air and breathing it. Here, we don't see the interior soot. We keep coughing and blame it on others, who are coughing as violently as we are. Then we go through complications and feel traumatized by them. Now the wound, the hurt, becomes us. Not that we have pain; we *become* pain.

A self-applied Band-Aid, the way Colin does it, in adult language, is giving and taking the love we yearn for, as a magical healing force. It's the balm for the incomprehensible booboo.

SEARCHING FOR LIGHTS IN BUDAPEST

We were on an East European tour with an emphasis on visiting sites related to one of the most atrocious beastly human acts in history: The Holocaust.

Being a poor, careless reader, I had completely missed that aspect in the itinerary. I cry easily and cursed myself for going on a holiday that was going to make me cry. My pastime is enjoying curiosity and discovering goodness and beauty in the unknown.

There was plenty of that, too. Maybe it was even more highlighted being side by side with a horrific reality.

An underground salt mine in Krakow, Poland, build in the thirteenth century, deserves elevation to a world wonder. Kafka's residence in Prague was a tiny cave converted to a charming boutique.

My favourite experience was arriving at town squares, lit colourfully at night, inviting locals and tourists with live music and busy restaurants. From a distance, they looked like a musical jewel box.

We arrived in Budapest in the early afternoon. Our tour guide gave us a brief description about its history, being formed of two cities; Buda and Pest (pronounced Pesht) in ancient times, attracting all form of conquerors, including Turks and Communists, and finally becoming the capital of the liberated Hungary in the early twentieth century.

Then she left us on our own until the next day.

I decided to do my usual walking all over the city and find my musical jewel box. A few in the group, witnessing my enthusiasm, wanted to join me and, before too long, we were about a dozen or more, all relying on my exuberance not knowing that I walked with no map in my hand—nor in my mind. Just forging along and asking the locals: "Please, how should I get to the centre of the city?"

I think when some of them started to have second thoughts about their decision, it was already too late.

After a few minutes of late summer afternoon fading sunshine, which allowed us to see the beautiful, lush Danube roaring between Buda and Pest, and nestling one of the most magnificent castles in Europe, a storm started. The rain was relentless and the winds were gaining stamina. Always hoping for the best, I thought the rain would stop soon. My thoughtful tour mates had no umbrella. As for me, I very rarely carry one.

We all took shelter beside a wall ornamented with carved figures from the distant past. I kept asking passersby about the centre of the city, but nobody paid attention. Until one person with a perfect Canadian or New York accent said, "Just follow me!"

He was a short, athletically built, youngish-looking man who was stylishly attired in summer shorts and a shirt, with a neat haircut, so pale blonde he almost looked like an albino, holding the leash of a large white dog. By this time, darkness had descended and the streetlights were on.

I gave the good news to the rest of the group and started to walk with him in the crowded large streets of this magnificent capital. The walk took at least half an hour, with the rain waxing and waning, and the group following two or three feet behind us.

I expressed my surprise regarding his perfect English. He told me he had been in Toronto until five years ago. He was a classical cellist born in Hungary, transported to the United States in early childhood; his parents, now diseased, were fleeing communism. After completing his education and working for several classical orchestras, he went to Toronto and worked in the same capacity producing his solos. There, he had received a letter from the Hungarian government that his parents' properties had been cleared and he'd decided to come to Hungary and fell in love with it.

He soon had a place in the Budapest Philharmonic Orchestra. He married a Hungarian tour guide and was divorced, with no children with her. But he had many children from different women in different places! His transparency was like we were old friends. We did not exchange names.

By this time, we arrived in the centre of the city, we were drenched. All the summer umbrellas around the courtyard had been blown away or taken away. There was no evidence of a jewel box or music. He guided us to enter a hotel in the courtyard, thinking we were going to eat. One look at our disappointed faces made it clear that nobody had any intention to make the time nicer now that we were properly sheltered. I approached the group and said it would be courteous if we invited the gentleman for a drink. The silent wave of disagreement was so loud that I retreated. They wanted to go back to our hotel at once.

As soon as the kind cellist heard that, he said he would get us in the cab, as it is rare for anybody to speak English there and, because of the rain, it would be very difficult to get one. He did put all of us, every three or four, in different cabs that he either called with his phone or hailed. I did not see anybody expressing the slightest gratitude. I was in a state of shock as these people were ordinarily a polite society.

In the hotel when we joined for a few minutes before parting, I asked the reason for their behaviour. They said they had thought the gentleman was a hobo or a vagrant! They were too frightened to be with him but followed because they were also frightened of being lost. But after he kindly put them in cabs, they had relaxed. I told them who he was and they looked at me skeptically.

The next morning the aforementioned group had chosen a different tour and I did not see them until dinnertime. Like a bunch of excited children, they gathered around me and said that the gentleman who had helped us the night before had come to the bus tour early in the morning bringing a cup of coffee for our tour guide, who told them he was her ex-husband and a very friendly, kind gentleman, a classical cellist in the philharmonic orchestra.

All my self-doubt disappeared, as I had questioned my judgment and even questioned why should I have believed him. He was all the lights in Budapest, a musical jewel box. I cry when I feel tender.

MOST BEAUTIFUL SCULPTURES ARE POEMS SET IN BRONZE

There was a time I had to visit every museum and art gallery that came my way, sometimes repeatedly, to the extent that our children knew the map of our path.

Then a distaste set in and later it matured into active avoidance. I felt that I was missing the whole world by focusing on what had become the rock stars in art and history. The glittering things had robbed me from seeing the extraordinary beauty that was spread all over.

Early in this phase in our nearly yearly visit to New York, I had seen the statue of a pregnant goat in the courtyard of the Museum of Modern Art, MOMA. The courtyard was free of charge.

The darkened bronze "She Goat" by Picasso was a solitary feature there. I would sit beside it and marvel at its story. So pregnant that the lower abdominal part and gorged nipples were almost touching the ground, while the body of the goat seemed to have no flesh on it. Its ribs were protruding through the back and neck, as if one life had to be finished by nurturing before another one could start. The face of the goat looked serene in anticipation. The story etched in bronze told the beauty of nurturing.

Over the years, other objects of art were added to the courtyard, but She Goat was the only one that would stir me. In my most recent visit to MOMA's courtyard, no longer free of charge, my friend Shohreh was also excited to meet the humble masterpiece. The courtyard looked like a zoo of cluttered art pieces and the pregnant goat was no longer in its fixed spot. We were told that it had been removed because there was an exhibition going on in another part of the museum. We would wait until She Goat was released from captivity.

I had zero interest in an African safari when in South Africa, although it's supposed to be the highlight of the tour. Waiting for half an hour in a van, in absolute silence, in the magnificent Kruger National Park for two lions to show up for an early morning walk brought no sense of anticipation for me.

But in another part in Kruger National Park, I felt breathless by the statue of two life-sized kudu bulls with their elaborate horns interlocked, one on top grounding the other, the work of Hennie Potgieter. The faces of the kudus were exhausted to the point of lifelessness. The title was "The Conquered Victor." The story etched in bronze was captivating. There was no winner in the war.

In a different site depicting the biological diversity of plants in this blessed land of fertility, I was entranced by another sculptor's work, "Cheetah Chasing the Buck," by Dylan Lewis. A life-sized cheetah was stretched almost to a straight line climbing a tree, with one front paw holding the back leg of a goat, also stretched to a straight line in the air, trying to escape. Like the former sculpture, the beauty, artistry and anatomical precision of bodies in motion were paled by the story etched in the bronze. What would you like to happen? For the hungry cheetah to get a morsel of its God-given food, or for the innocent goat's life to be spared? One's judgment is badly tested.

It reminded me of the Korean story when Weasel pleads with the hen not to hurt her babies out of anger, because Weasel has to eat the hen's brood not out of any hostility, but because nature has designated them as her food.

I was recounting the magnanimity of these sculptures to my friend Neil (formerly known as my son), and he responded, "Like a poem set in bronze."

I loved his phrase so much that I stole it.

HE LIVES ON

At age ninety-two, my former professor had lived a rich life, even considering massive hardships and a tragedy. But tender tears filled my heart reading about celebration of his life. I was grateful that I had met him, even briefly. He had left an enduring sense of gratitude in me, going back to a time when we knew practically nothing of each other except our names. So distant we stayed. I read it in a newspaper. So distant.

Standing on the edge of a precipice of life takes away all fears and illusions about death. There is nothing to look at. Nothing to contemplate. Nothing to entice curiosity. The eyes keep being diverted toward life. Every minutia takes a glittering existence of its own and fills one with a desire to get to know it. It is the mere sadness of leaving all these insignificant details and the magnanimous tapestry made of them. Being all our perception. Our illusion. What a beautiful thing to have illusion. It's so engaging.

The other side leaves no room for imagination. Nothing to latch onto.

Whatever we were told about "the other side" was based on creating a balance of power favouring those who were tightly grabbing existence in this life and did not want to share the benefits with the rest. "Leave the worldly to me, you will get your reward in heaven." Their greatest illusion was the possibility of interminable life. Eternity on this side was coveted. But they promised many good things upon our arrival on that "other side." Plus, eternal life.

While this small, ultra-smart group tried to disengage others from life, they missed out on life, too.

The holder of this self-defying thought gravitated toward religion. They used the available tools for salvation and a good life to alienate the rest from it. They projected their inner demons into frightening imagery on the blank screen of the other side, while fearfully grabbing life.

And just a simple look proves it. Across various points in human history, look at all the religious leaders living in the lap of luxury, from Egyptian priests who were supposed to get celestial favours to bargain with the other side for a better deal, to Buddhist priests loaded with gold, to representatives of Judaism, Christianity, Islam, and modern cults. Not a single average human can so vehemently deny the end of life.

Simply the end of life. Nothing within our grasp on the other side. Our brain is not made to understand that side. No puzzle to decipher. While at the side of life we are showered by unsolved and unsolvable problems.

My professor left the aroma of goodness in my existence. With no reward from me. He was not solicited to do so. It was a sheer coincidence that he was on my way.

At the height of my arrogance of youth, as a novice resident, when speaking out with no diplomacy was equal to personal dignity, I offended a big shot, specifically, an extremely fragile chief of service in the department of psychiatry of a hospital. I simply told him the hospital teaching was "very bad!" And it was. I was a junior resident and barely spoke English, and had close to zero knowledge of my field and much less of the world in general. But I was correct in that issue. All eight of my fellow residents shared the view. But I said it out loud.

At the end of six months, the chief of service, who had minimal contact with me, took the liberty of writing my evaluation report and, after a precise explanation of my wrongdoings, including endangering the lives of patients, requested my exclusion from further participation in residency. Now in this hospital we were allowed the least contact with the patients, most of them being private patients of the staff.

It was mandatory to sign the evaluation. To his utter disbelief, I refused.

I had started my second term of my second year at what is now called the Centre for Addiction and Mental Health and was then called the Clarke Institute of Psychiatry. The most advanced psychiatric hospital in Canada, it had seen a surge of new brilliant minds due to political upheavals in Quebec. Usually, it was McGill University in Montreal that benefited from a brain drain out of Toronto and the world in general. Now Toronto was becoming a hub, attracting academics. This grey, quiet city was deemed safe for the intellectuals who just wanted to make a living by academic means without politics.

One of these academics, in my mind the most brilliant one, was the director of education, Professor R. His biweekly or monthly lectures were solid and rich. Unpretentiously presenting highly relevant information was his focus. Most interesting of all for me was the breadth of his knowledge in all areas. One of his remarks that stayed in my thirsty brain was totally unrelated to psychiatry. It was purely about the economics of real life. In one of his talks for general residents and staff, I heard him say, "Psychiatry is a bag for you to beg!" It took me years to decipher this and value it truly. And I begged handsomely by it.

But this very valuable entity was generally feared by residents. The name of Professor R prompted fears of being kicked out of the program. I did not know him but for a few lectures, which I attended out of fear. But the name cast a dark shadow of indiscriminate injustice.

on that fateful day when my world collapsed after receiving my evaluation from the last hospital, in my mind I was rapidly collecting my meagre clothing from my tiny apartment, and buying my ticket back to my beloved country of birth. The cruelty was unbearable. I entered the Clarke Institute one final time to inform my supervisor of my imminent departure, to say a polite goodbye after a brief explanation.

While briskly crossing the hall to get to the elevator, I heard a loud bass voice from afar calling my name. Very disinterestedly, I looked toward the voice. It was Professor R. He had stopped and was gesturing to me to come toward him.

As I approached him, he said, "Dr. GhaemMaghami, what's happened? I've never seen you so sad!" I was shocked. How could he know me? A lowly resident. Never introduced. We had never exchanged a word. As far as I knew, I was invisible to him. Had tried hard.

And he knew my name and my hallmark laughter and giggle. A joyful creature, carefree and cocky.

I had nothing to lose anymore. I told him exactly what had happened. To this man who was supposed to be the number-one enemy of all residents.

Professor R, without batting an eyelash, responded: "You are not going anywhere. You are one of our best residents. I'll look after it. Just go and look after your patients."

I never received such a compliment again in my life.

The big shot's evaluation had been pulverized.

I never thanked Professor R for his unconditional kindness. I never expressed my amazement for his keen observation, picking my sadness from the corner of the hall without any prior personal contact.

Did he die? Did he leave life?

His gift to me pervaded my practice. And if I could have offered someone something remotely similar to what he gave me, I would be very happy. He lives on.

SOMETIMES A CERTIFICATE IS NOT JUST A CERTIFICATE!

Among all the negative and positive features courtesy of Covid-19, many are intertwined.

Travelling around the world up to five times a year came to a sudden halt for me. It opened up vistas leading to opportunities that had been overlooked up to then. Seeing more of thriving Toronto, for example. A baby that, in my eyes, grew from a grey patch to a cosmopolitan arena.

Watching salmon spawning had been a must for me, but thanks to my enthusiastic friends, it finally became a reality early in the fall.

The morning was crisp with a chill. High above us, a paling and yet cheery sun was entertained by celestial turquoise overcoming silver clouds. On our way, a long row of birch trees that had been a minor attraction in summer were demurely showing off their translucent red leaves dancing in an autumn breeze. What a feast.

We made it to Humber River and Etienne Brûlée Park. It was leafy and green, mixed with the impermanence of hues from yellow gold to crimson red leaves carpeting the ground at one side of the river, where spectators were gathering. On the other bank stood a row of high-rise residential buildings.

People were either watching or taking shots of high-flying salmon leaping over the man-made dam.

Meandering in the gentle water close to the dam were a few men in fishing gear, trying to catch salmon. What an ideal fishing expedition, with the slowed-down school of female salmon in shallow water going against the current. Of course, the amateur fishermen let the salmon go.

Did Etienne Brulé ever watch spawning salmon? After all, he was one of the first settlers blended with Canada's native population and studied their languages and cultures. Unfortunately, his penchant for the fur trade made him betray his adoptive tribe. He was killed by the Hurons at the tender age of forty-one. I am sure the Hurons taught him a lot about fish and their natural cycles. Alas, those natives have been betrayed over and over. Mi'kmaq lobster fishermen have been attacked and their tools trashed and set on fire in Nova Scotia. And, for years, contaminated water has damaged their lives in Ontario and elsewhere.

Watching spawning salmon is not for the weak of heart. The brave salmon with large bellies swims from the ocean toward the river in search of gravel beds to lay their eggs.

It seems that the gravel beds are not too far before where water picks up speed, cascading down from the dam.

One sees the large black body of the salmon speeding up to jump and throw itself over the dam, and rarely succeeding. Those who survive the multiple traumas and injuries, who can throw themselves over the dam, will spawn. Once eggs are laid, the body of the salmon will disintegrate to edible form for the newly hatched baby salmons. A mother sacrificing herself for her babies could not be more heroic . . . or tragic.

Once back home, I took a bath in preparation for my afternoon work. A chill, a few sneezes, and a runny nose portended a cold. I wore warmer clothes and informed my friends of my symptoms. In times of Corona, this was simple courtesy. Every cold could be the beginning of Covid-19. As practically normally occurring cold had disappeared during Covid activity. It was strongly suggested that I get a test. Indeed, I was registered online by my lovely friend for the earliest possible test in three days.

With great resistance and almost symptom-free but for a wispy voice, I succumbed to the prevailing social norm, feeling sure I just had a short-lived cold, and underwent the ordeal. A long line, albeit moving rapidly, a few bureaucratic stops asking the same questions over and over again, being set up in internet – and, finally, a less than 10 second probe of a nostril and a split second of unbearable pain. It was over and done with.

Four days earlier watching salmon spawning in Etienne Brulé Park, each time a salmon hit the flat rock of the dam, I felt a cringe and a pang of pain all over my body. But the pain induced by the probe for Covid-19 was closer to labour pain.

I walked with delight along Avenue Road, cleared from regular pedestrians, bereft of ambiance because of closed restaurants and most businesses, emptied of all summer flowers, and with only occasional trees. Over my head, the turquoise sky had yielded to silver and rain-drops were gently falling. I was celebrating life. Breathing the clean air washed by a light rain.

The appearance of a COVID-19 "negative" certificate on my com-puter monitor the next day brought an excitement and happiness more intense than the achievement of my combined MD and FRCPC designations. Both of them opened windows toward unfathomable responsibilities and perils.

My Covid-19 certificate was pure relief. I could see my family and friends. And I had not transmitted Covid-19 to anyone.

HALLOWE'EN HAS ITS OWN TRIALS AND TRIBULATIONS

No Hallowe'en in 2020

The news was passing around with urgency. The cancelation of Canadian Thanksgiving dinner was taken with a stiff upper lip by the majority. Maybe a quiet, rather secret small gathering of just a few was acceptable.

Everybody was emotionally parched and starved to have a few minutes like the good old days around the table with loved ones.

Even those with a low tolerance for human vocal ambiance now found it nostalgic of the far, far past.

But the cancellation of Hallowe'en was like transgressing into the domain of innocent, defenceless creatures. Sacrosanct.

A lack of Hallowe'en decorations as it was coming closer was heavy, even for me.

I have no aptitude for frightful scenes. And some I am appalled by. Like mutilated bloody hands, independent fingers on the move, severed heads. Yet collectively, I like Hallowe'en decoration.

Sometimes creativity is admirable.

And then children coming with homemade costumes and masks or dressed up by purchased costumes attributed to famous characters.

And even some parents with matching outfits with their children, smirking behind their masks, encouraging their children to say thank you. All bring a transient pure joy to candy-giving.

Once my children had passed the excitement of candy gathering, Hallowe'en became a task for me. Making sure that there would be enough candy down to the final teenagers who were last to arrive and always in a group and some with no mask or costume. Actually, I liked it. Adolescence is so transient that it could be considered a mask by itself.

On this particular Hallowe'en, my anticipation of bell ringing and seeing the youngest children first was not fulfilled. Nobody rang the bell or knocked on the door. There was no group giggling on the other side of the door saying, "Trick or treat!"

By 7 p.m., I went to the front door and saw a few children with an adult at the other side of the street. Illuminated by my front door in the vast dark, I waved at them and they ran away. I realized that they were not prepared for a real witch!

I learned my lesson. I stood coolly inside in nail-biting intensity, and left the door open. Soon one actually walked in! Fearing that my chocolate bars may not go, I kept giving them away in bulk. I got far more teenagers in a short while. News of a generous witch had spread fast.

Almost all my candies were gone. I felt victorious!

And I developed better methods to market my candy-giving feast.

In Covid time the void of Hallowe'en was big. Indeed, it was worse than having no Thanksgiving dinner.

Hallowe'en is such a communal experience, its cultish origin notwithstanding, bringing adults to the wondrous world of children, sharing the effervescent youth for such a short time.

ITALIANS HAVEN'T CHANGED, MY FRIEND!

I have been lucky with my friends—each bringing wisdom and beauty into my life, along with, at hard times, precious badly needed support. Friendship is a work of nature, lowest maintenance and highest yield. With a pretext of zero expectation, a lot is gained by just being in company of each other, fearlessly transparent and honest.

Mariam and I met at the bedsides of patients, beleaguered by incomprehensible human afflictions we were supposed to understand and manage. While I was still dreaming of discovery and invention, Mariam was keenly in touch with human pain and was using healing power invested in her at the service of humanity.

Numerous times Mariam has chuckled sweetly and understandably at my sheer ignorance, while, with a few simple words, taken off my blinkers.

We have travelled together for conferences and managed to include some sight-seeing. Some required using local busses on numerous occasions on almost unsafe roads, like visiting Oedipus's grave in Thebes, a small Greek town rich with mythology. Somehow, I had expected a shrine for this man whose life was woven tragically from birth and had been elevated as a pivotal point in our understanding of humans through Freud's power of imagination. And here around this nondescript pile of dirt there was no sign of even a grave.

Two Greek teenagers were sitting on this heap, under the shade of large, spreading olive trees, holding hands and whispering those sweet words of young love that have no meaning in any language but which we eternally cherish and yearn for.

Cruelly, I interrupted this serenade of nightingales and asked, "Would you please tell us where Oedipus's grave is?" I knew even if they did not know English they would for sure know Oedipus. The young girl, about fourteen, with no perturbation, stretched her free hand and pointed to where we were standing. There was a barely noticeable hole among other holes. I said, "Oh, almost no grave! Is it because he did bad things? At the end even blinded himself!"

To my amazement, she responded, "No bad, no good. A tragedy!" At that moment I wished my children were Greek teenagers! So erudite by birth.

Mariam chuckled at my thoughts.

A few years later I took my children on a European journey, following a path I had gone as a single twenty-six-year-old, all by myself: France, Italy, Greece, Germany, Austria, and Switzerland. I was talking to Mariam about the trip and comparing the two. One significant difference was that Italian men had changed. "Mariam, you may not believe it, but Italy has become safe! On my first trip, at every step, an Italian man would come forward and ask me to have dinner or lunch with him, uttering, 'Multi bella, multi bella!' And how uncomfortable I felt ignoring those handsome, persistent louts! And in this recent trip, not one Italian man even looked at me. You see, Mariam, Italian men have changed!"

Mariam's chuckle was relentless, but she finally managed to say: "My dear friend, Italians have not changed. *We* have changed." And noticing my blank expression, she had to add, "We are not young anymore. And with three children in tow?!"

Did she have to be so honest?

No Kisses under
the 2020 Mistletoe

Xmas was coming full force. Mostly in my mind. Except for a sizeable snowfall and whiteness, the external world was reaffirming its non-existence. Even the music, the pervasive, uncontainable message heralding it, was scarce on regular radio stations.

The advertisements were all virtual. Pick-up places. Curbside pick-ups. Deliveries. Amazon.

Store windows were frozen in time. Some from summer, with lively, coloured bare-skin cuts. Many little stores were out of business for good, just waiting to be cleaned out, their windows dusty and insides dark. That included hair salons and manicure parlours.

A few that opened after reduced restriction for the fall soon had to retreat, their fall fashion lifeless in display windows. Hair products and nail polishes once more were gathering dust, this time with no promised opening day.

Brave restaurants fighting for their livelihood went full-fledged with Xmas decorations, observing all protocols of distancing, and masked staff were urged to close.

Patios that had been erected with outdoor heating facilities had to retreat, too. For a short time, it triggered hope that, from now on, winters in Toronto would be equipped like Copenhagen, with patios all along busy streets.

The Xmas convention of leaving for warmer places or ski hills was eliminated. Lockdown was getting tighter due to reports of an advancing enemy. An invisible enemy that was leaving death as its footprint that would not allow even the most defiant among us to defy it.

Covid was progressing. As had been predicted. Predicted in 2015! A flu virus with mutative power not seen before. But even everyday announcements about the increased number of infections were still received in surprise. Revealing our hope that, by some miracle, we would wake up from this nightmare. And get back to our comfortable reality. Had it been that good, our pre-Covid reality? We were marred by concepts of "enemy," "Make America great again," "us versus them," people losing their lives to drunk drivers, people dying from a winter flu despite vaccination, contaminated water damaging generations of our natives, plane crashes, indefatigable climate change, air pollution, people forced out of their native lands and drowned in cruel seas in search of a safe earth, and on and on.

Covid, however has had its own gifts. The regular flu seems to be out. It gave a sense of equality to the human race. It crossed all made-up barriers. It gave us lots of time and scared us with its imminent termination of life. It felt like we were all trying to be contained in Noah's ship until elusive safety arrived.

But at times keeping civil did not come easily. Misinformation about the young being resistant to it raised the ire of the young not wanting to be restricted to protect the elderly who'd already had their share of living. It gave us a chance to see our humanity on the brink. Who gets vaccinated first? Our teeth became sharp. Even knowing the vaccination would not be the ultimate protection.

With all respect for common sense I tried to take advantage of every available breadcrumb of pleasure reminiscent of a freshly made loaf of bread of formerly easily available fun. All easy fun that at no time I had taken for granted. Togetherness, family, friends, health, my work, nature, sharing life with others in its simplest form, and . . . cherished solitude.

With friends on our long walks we sat on stone benches in parks, drinking our coffees we'd purchased from a take-out. Watched and fed birds in Edwards Gardens and Sunnybrook Park. Vexed poetics watching the gorging autumn creeks after a dry summer. Enjoyed the changing colour of leaves that sometimes happened within hours, bringing a novel landscape among the trees. We got the chance to bow to the grandeur of nature by watching the spawning of salmons. Just enjoying whatever was available at the moment. Isn't life just Now, with due consideration for what we learned Yesterday, and respecting the unknown of Tomorrow?

Xmas is an adopted feature in my life. It's another cultish occasion to bring people together to share life's bounties. And to look at good and bad in seamless way. The harmony of dissonance. Like all other things with me, I improvise at Xmas, too. Adding a delicious Persian dish to a traditional meal. Some me and some tradition. Isn't life simply our interpretation of facts that will remain forever elusive to us?

So, I went on with my Xmas arrangement. The duller the real world, the more colourful my Xmas would be. A fresh tree, as usual, is a must. Every single decoration was with the thought of bringing a smile to one of my grandchildren's faces. The glowing angels, the singing bird, the wiggling Santa, the stocking with the inscription "I've Been Good."

And the mistletoe was installed in its usual place: the door frame of the entrance to the dining room. It had stored the beautiful scenes of my sons kissing their future wives under it. I could still taste the deliciousness of fresh love. My own first under a different mistletoe long ago. And going back and forth to get more. How romantic. I kept thinking: who will have a kiss under mistletoe this Xmas? each time I entered the dining room and it accidentally hit my head.

The artistic friend made her usual highly decorated freshly baked gingerbread house. What a joy when grandchildren steal a chocolate or candy from it, looking intently for their parents' approval. Only one! Your teeth don't like sugar.

The aroma of sage and thyme infiltrated the house.

The turkey was juicy and the stuffing was out of this world, splattered by a Persian berry. Even the smallest turkey is too much for only three guests. Never mind that there will be some take-out for absentees. Xmas music filled the house to make up for the shortage of ambiance.

I said my usual prayer before starting to eat: "God thank you for all the family and friends and good food. Please give us more."

And I kept being hit by the mistletoe each time I entered the dining room, passing in oblivion underneath it.

Despite the absence of kisses under the mistletoe, I am hoping for an Easter Bunny with lots of eggs.

SOMETIMES A SMILE MAY NOT JUST BE A SMILE

Freud painstakingly tried to uncover the meaning of human behaviour in particular repeated patterns, in order to understand the root of dysfunction and pain. After years of such academic devotion, with an extensive focus on sexual undertones, some of his followers, trying to emulate the mentor and noticing that Freud rarely let his cigar separate from his lips, brought it to his attention, hoping the master interpreter would reveal some insight into his cancer-enhancing habit. They were dumbfounded when Freud responded, "Sometimes a cigar is just a cigar!" This phrase has become a leitmotiv on occasions when a psychological hypocrisy is suspected.

In late summer 2015, I enjoyed the good fortune of having a personal tour to the Balkans, as usual with no map or plan. What had triggered the interest, like many of my other tours, was a simple coincidence, which had gotten my attention relentlessly.

A person had written in the travel section of *The Globe and Mail* that she enjoyed travelling to a little picturesque ancient port town called Piran, rarely known to tourists, and still not very much known. That's always a trigger for me.

I went to my reliable friend Google and found Piran sitting at the tip of a little country called Slovenia, long before Melania Trump brought it to the map.

I had to see it. And thus began the Balkan trip. I planned to get to Piran starting from Bulgaria, and to make a full circle by coming back to Sofia via all the other Balkan countries.

Sofia and a few ancient towns in Bulgaria were beautiful, and by third day, I was in Bucharest and a few small towns in Romania, all with their own beauty, including the village in Transylvania where the real castle for the mythical Dracula stands on a story-like hill. In both countries, still living with the trauma of the post-war impoverished economy, people were kind and polite and thirsty for tourists. I had become accustomed to leaving my iPhone charging on the patio of a little restaurant while trying to get an address, reassured by the proprietor that it was absolutely safe.

The next country was Serbia. Belgrade was far more prosperous and yet tourism was dead. Still, there was a significant difference here with the people. Some Serbians smiled!

I had not noticed how very rarely—if at all—people in Bulgaria and Romania smiled.

The first service person in Serbia who smiled while answering my question suddenly made me aware that I'd experienced some smile deficiency for a few days. The smile was pale compared with those of Thai people and even North Americans, but—still—it was a smile. I kept encountering this with Serbians despite the language barrier, hoping to compensate for the smile deprivation I had suffered.

My plan to go to Piran became complicated.

Due to political issues rooted in economic disputes, the transport was frequently switched from a straight line to a zigzag route. In the Belgrade train station, I chose a large, sunlit patio facing the upcoming train, a two-minute walk away.

I had half an hour. I put my iPhone on a little round metal table with one chair, adjacent to the restaurant, close to an outlet, and plugged it in.

Then I went into the restaurant to order a beer. The cheapest way to get a chair and time is to order a house beer or wine. Not water. I usually don't talk, just point, when I know language is a serious barrier. And most of the time I can pass as a local.

When I came to the entrance I faced a beautiful sunny day. I became all smiles, seeing people, practically all local, sitting here and there on the patios of restaurants in the train station. I smiled at the beautiful world, and barely noticed a gentleman standing a few metres away, looking in my direction. Our eyes met in a blink.

I sat down at my little table and the cheap beer was put in front of me.

Suddenly, I noticed that the aforementioned gent—who was around my age, very good looking, and nicely dressed—was standing near my table and smiling shyly, glancing at me. And, in a minute, the proprietor had pulled a chair up to my table, and put an expensive beer on it. The gentleman sat down!

What do you say before you have said hello? There had been a misunderstanding.

I swallowed my smile and asked the proprietor politely, "Is this gentleman going to sit here?" The proprietor whispered just a word to him and he almost flew away! Taking his beer with him.

Both had been under the impression that I was Serbian or at least a Balkan, and that my smile was an invitation to have him as a company while waiting for the train! I would have loved it if I could speak a word of Serbian or if he could a word of English. What a great opportunity it could have been! But I don't like long-distance relationships!

I became much more conscious of my random smiling after that. Sometimes, a smile may not be taken just as a smile. Or maybe I am a psychological hypocrite.

I finally arrived at Piran by way of a convoluted passage. It was as beautiful as the person in *The Globe and Mail* had described it: an ancient beauty with all the modern amenities, and with little tourism. I managed to put my foot in the Adriatic Sea with a big smile.

Sarajevo, where Turks and Austrians forever face off, makes up for all the other Balkan countries, by attracting huge numbers of tourists. But the smiles here were still scarce.

About the Author

Dr. Toghra GhaeMaghami is a practicing psychiatrist in Toronto where she is blessed by her children, grandchildren, family and friends. And a treasure of precious patients.